Makarska

Makarska

a novel by

Jim Bartley

INSOMNIAC PRESS

Copyright © 2015 by Jim Bartley

All rights reserved. No part of this publication may be reproduced, stored in a retrieval system or transmitted, in any form or by any means, without the prior written permission of the publisher or, in the case of photocopying or other reprographic copying, a licence from Access Copyright, 1 Yonge Street, Suite 1900, Toronto, ON M5E 1E5

Library and Archives Canada Cataloguing in Publication

Bartley, Jim, 1952-, author
Makarska / Jim Bartley.

Issued in print and electronic formats.
ISBN 978-1-55483-149-4 (pbk.).--ISBN 978-1-55483-161-6 (html)

I. Title.

PS8553.A777M35 2015   C813'.54   C2015-902379-3
                                   C2015-902380-7

The publisher gratefully acknowledges the support of the Canada Council, the Ontario Arts Council, and the Department of Canadian Heritage through the Canada Book Fund.

Printed and bound in Canada

Insomniac Press
520 Princess Avenue, London, Ontario, Canada, N6B 2B8
www.insomniacpress.com

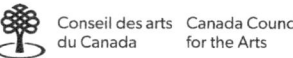

For Brian

1

The woman is showing him pictures. Pero knows her, but he doesn't know how or why. She has an album of photos from his childhood.

"This is Mostar, *Tata*. The old bridge. Do you remember?"

Of course he remembers the Mostar bridge. And there beside him is his mother and his Uncle Todor, whose house they stayed at. The summers were hot, hotter than Sarajevo.

The woman flips the page. Here he is (she tells him) at age six, in front of the Sarajevo apartment house with his mother. They both wear dark wool coats, his mother's with a fur collar. There is the muddy fender of a car to one side, and behind them snow heaped against a wall. Pero doesn't need her to tell him about this photo either. He knows it, knows the street, remembers the facade of the building. Under the photo are handwritten letters, white on the black paper: *Pero 6 Despićeva*. His mother is smiling broadly. He is simply staring with a wide-eyed, vaguely frightened look.

Again a new page, now with photos that he can't place, though there is something almost familiar. The pictures please him. The woman wants him to remember these people, this place that she calls Makarska. "The sea," she says. "Our summer house." Over and over the same words.

The woman is saying she is his daughter, Kristina. Yes. He hears this from her. A memory that comes and disappears again. Like a person coming out of fog and passing by back into the fog behind. Turn around and there is nothing. He looks at her face. His daughter. Well. If she says so, but she seems far too old for that.

"But you are old, *Tata*. You are seventy-seven."

"No, not possible."

"It's true."

"You say this. That does not mean it's true."

She makes him look in a mirror. It's true that he looks not like himself.

He is moving to the stairs and up, turning at the landing, now this way, along the hall, now turning into the bathroom. He opens his pants and pulls it out and waits. Sighs. Push. Out in thin bursts. And here is the man behind him.

"Daddy, you have been here for twenty minutes."

They sometimes call him *Daddy* in English,

sometimes *Tata*, like back home.

"Daddy?"

"I'm not finished."

"Focus."

"Leave me be."

"Come on now, I think you're done. Dinner is ready."

He's on the sofa. Who is the man opposite? Another person he sees here, familiar. A family person, staring at a small object that he taps with his thumbs.

"Who are you?"

The young man looks up long enough to say, "Mirza." Then back to the tapping.

"Mirza."

"That's me. You're my Grampa. My *Deda*. Pero."

"I know I am Pero."

He does know that he is Pero, even if he forgets sometimes. He forgets things about these people who keep explaining to him. He forgets that he has a forgetting problem. People in the house help him. They tell him he's in a new country. They show him the newspaper, the news on the television. He remembers all the things from before, the important things: his parents, the Despićeva Street apartment. Wartime is prominent: the Partisans. Fighting the Germans and Ustashas and all the rest. He remembers

Mara: falling for her, going away together on the train. They say she died, but he has no recall of that.

They also say that he was a professor in England, for many years. He knows that England is a country. He looks at the books beside him on the shelf, the gold letters on the spines. The one with his name right there on the cover. He is Pero Banjac. History is in this book. But he doesn't need a book or old pictures to remember his father who was killed in Perućica, or his mother who died in her own bed in Sarajevo with himself and his sister beside her. She died because the war meant they could not have the drug that would cure her.

He's feeling sleepy now. He's remembering the Brigades, his friend Šaban, the wrecked truck and the river, and the boy.

2

Mirza has seen the old x-ray image. The fragment of metal in his grandfather's head looks like a jagged cashew nut. Lying quietly under the sheets at noon on a Monday, hiding from the bright June sun, he thinks about headspace: the hot brain-mousse in there. He feels mentally acute in the way he sometimes does just after waking up. His mind is processing his surroundings, his yesterday, his possible today, at peak efficiency. Strange, because physically he feels like crap. A hangover can sharpen perceptions even while it puts distracting sensations in the way. Right now his forehead, the space behind it, seems too full. A clog of wet bone. If he moves his head too quickly, the soggy bonemass slides and bumps inside his skull.

He wrestled in the pissy weeds by the river with Teo and Danny. He got so drunk he lost track of things, of where he began and ended, of arms and legs, who they belonged to. Danny disappeared. Teo walked, dragged, him home. It was crazy, like high school again, like the residual teenager got released for a night. At least he didn't throw up, not that he can remember.

A wet feather and sleep and spilt booze smell. Mirza's mother does not wash bedding now. She seems to be letting things go, but if he says this to her, he knows he will suffer consequences. He maybe should do the laundry himself. He sometimes washes his own clothes — more often lately due to circumstances. But it seems he has reached the age of twenty-five and not yet washed his own sheets. Maybe it's time. Kristina is at work. She looked at him so sadly, distantly, when Teo wrestled him in and dropped him on the couch and they talked about him or something while he slumped into the cushions. He could wash the sheets and not say anything, remake the bed, and she would see this miracle and ask, and he could shrug, yes, no big deal. On the other hand, it would set a precedent.

Mirza and Teo are artists. They actually have degrees — well, Teo two-thirds of a degree. Why they both still live with their mothers, instead of in a crumbling Queen West walk-up, is largely economic, but it needs to change. Danny talks about "the absurdity factor." He was the one who showed up with the whiskey last night, a big bottle of Bushmills. He is one hundred per cent Canadian, but Teo and Mirza share an immigrant connection. Their fathers fought in Bosnia, so they know absurd and know that Danny is really just dancing on the surface.

Last night they told Danny about the final Yugo car to roll off the line in Serbia, and the bidding for it online, and Danny said he would maybe put in a bid of one dollar, which was probably the main cause of the rolling around in the weeds. They wanted him to pay for this insult to a truly iconic specimen of automotive engineering. Mixed in with everything else was a stupid but endless argument Mirza had with Teo about art versus illustration. The ganging up on Danny may have been partly about that. Danny still carries a high-school taint. It may be time to let the friendship slide.

Mirza's father, Adem, has gone back to his old friends in Sarajevo. They have some kind of deal going with house construction. It was what Adem did before the war and again in Canada, even though he has a degree in mechanical engineering. Now back on his own territory again, he claims to be a bigger boss. The plan is to make money and bring it back to Toronto — the complete reverse of the usual immigrant cash flow. Whether Adem will actually come back to his wife and son is the main question. Kristina seems to consider the whole thing just one more Bosnian scam. If you're connected with the right people, you can get rich fast in BiH. Adem's attitude is that as a siege survivor he deserves a piece of the guilt money still being doled out by all the foreigners who failed to stop the Serbs. He called them the *peacefakers* in the war and still does. Mirza basically agrees with his dad, but he has known for years how risky it is to say this to his Toronto friends, and anyway, most people have forgotten about Sarajevo.

The occasional times that Canadians used to ask Adem about his war, usually in a bar after a drink or two, he would pause and stare at the floor, then look them straight in the eye and say simply, "Bad." He had a routine. He would look down at his hand, like it was not a part of him. The hand would float up and place itself over his heart, and then the fingers would slowly clutch together and pull away. Gazing at the beating heart torn from his chest, he would take a pensive drag on his cigarette. People generally did not ask more questions after that. The ones who did heard in detail about the peacefakers, and then things sometimes got tense.

Mirza's Grandpa Pero is clinically demented thanks to his shrapnel wound from the siege. Twelve years after they left Sarajevo behind, sponsored by the Canadian uncle who'd known Yugoslavia only as a visitor, Mirza's mother finally decided it was her brother's turn to billet their disabled dad. Uncle Alex had an empty bedroom, flexible work hours — she thought he ought to be ready to take a share of the family grief into his roomy house. Now Pero has been with Alex almost a year. Mirza has to admit it's been a relief not having his grandpa in the cramped bungalow on Gamble Avenue: his restless shuffling from room to room, his recycled monologues, his weak bladder. And his mother's complaining and shouting.

Mirza remembers Pero from before and after the shrapnel wound, mixed up with all his other childhood memories from the siege. A few years after Mirza's grandma died of cancer, still only in her fifties, Grandpa Pero retired from his university career in England and returned to the city he'd grown up in, the same city his British-born daughter had married herself into with Adem. Pero arrived in Sarajevo just a few months before the war began and brought a shopping bag full of English goodies — chocolate, hard candies, fancy nuts, little fruitcakes in red cellophane. The cakes sat untouched until war came, then they were rationed out by Kristina.

Mirza remembers that Pero brought some new tensions into their family life. Like his father, his grandpa did not help much around the apartment. When he went out for his daily walks, Kristina would release her pent-up frustrations on Mirza and Adem. The good side was that Mirza sometimes went out on these walks with his grandad. They would sit in a café, watching the crowds in Vase Miskina, or if the day was mild, catch some sun on a park bench. Sometimes they even saw a film. It was the sort of family activity his parents had fallen away from.

Then it was wartime. Pero took on necessary things like helping Adem to get water, but soon the water was far away, somewhere up in the hills, so he was retired from that. When Adem was gone to the front lines, Mirza's mother or the neighbours got the water. Mirza and his grandpa took on the task of washing the dishes when Kristina came in exhausted from lugging the heavy jugs — but she stopped them from this, saying they wasted water and didn't properly clean things.

Then the shrapnel flew in through the kitchen window and into Pero's forehead. He nearly died in Koševo Hospital, but didn't, and he came home to be cared for. And then the war was over and Uncle Alex helped them come to Canada. Now, it's Alex's turn to take charge of the old man and put up with his strange ways.

Mirza knows what his mother suffered. He knows less what his father suffered because it happened out in the battle zones and Adem has never talked in any detail about it, but his wounds are obvious. He has a small bald patch, a scooped-out depression, above his left ear. He has entry and exit scars from a bullet that passed through his thigh muscle, barely grazing the bone. He's missing two toes of his left foot from being shot accidentally by a fellow soldier (which is the wound he will talk about, because it's a joke — he is still good friends with the man who shot him).

Mirza was thirteen when the war ended. During the siege, his days were a mix of terrifying and boring but an extremely stressful boring. For almost four years he spent most of his time cooped up in the apartment or passing through the dusty yard between theirs and the next building. If no shells were coming in, he was allowed to run across to visit his friend Kemo, but playing in the yard itself was usually forbidden. Mirza doesn't spend a lot of time thinking back on all of this, consciously dwelling on it. His occasional nightmares are not conscious, but he can sometimes keep them away by telling himself at bedtime that he will only dream good things.

His mother went out for water. She was almost home when she heard a shell coming in, and she ran into the vestibule of a small apartment house. A bomb landed in the street, and she heard screams, then later she had to witness the dead once the wounded were taken away and she was brave enough to go out and look for her water jugs. She found the jugs in the street where she'd dropped them, still full. There was a burning bus and pools of blood and parts of bodies, and she saw a mask lying on the ground. Then she realized that it was a face, not a mask. She said it looked like the grey-bearded face of the baker they'd always bought their bread from, in the days when people used to go out in the mornings for fresh bread. There were only holes where the baker's eyes had been. She could see pavement through the holes, she said, which is why she'd thought it was a mask.

Now Mirza sits in front of his laptop in the kitchen, freshly showered and coffee-buzzed. He was probably around eleven years old when the baker was killed. He doesn't know if it happened before or after his grandfather's shrapnel wound. There were enough such days and events that it's now impossible to sort them out, but one prominent memory is his mother's absence to care for a sick friend in Grbavica, a nearby suburb. She was not herself when she came back. She couldn't sleep, she hardly ate. She had bouts of wailing and weeping, what seemed to Mirza the wildest sort of hysteria. What happened to her was not discussed — not then, and not since.

One recent night his mother was sitting on the couch with a glass of wine and she started talking, as if to herself, about the face on the sidewalk. Then her eyes changed, and she came back to the bungalow on Gamble Avenue. She sipped her wine and looked at her son, who survived everything to become a Canadian, with even a Canadian name, Mickey — simply a new spelling for Miki, his old schoolyard name. (If Canadian people ask, Mirza always says he's Canadian first. Privately, he's not sure.) This particular night was one of the times when his mother went missing, like she slipped out of present time. She slowly finished off her bottle of wine, crying silently for hours and watching some kind of movie in her head.

Mirza never watches that kind of movie. Memories just appear sometimes and are what they are. He observes them but doesn't think about them. His habit is to carry on like they belong outside him or to someone else, but lately this is changing. The memories seem more to be goading him, popping up like funhouse ghouls. On television he saw a retired general talking about Rwanda, what he'd witnessed there. He said it never left him: "It didn't happen in 1994. It happened this morning." Mirza understood exactly. Even the year was right.

In front of Mirza at the kitchen table is his new desktop photo, a shot of the Drina River gorge, the water a soft green like jade. The photo has come with an email from his father. Bosnia, Adem says in the message, is a beautiful country, one that Mirza barely saw as a child. Adem suggests that Mirza might want to spend some time getting to know his country, and what better way than in the Bosnian construction business — especially since he's jobless in Toronto. His father thinks the artist thing is a hobby and always will.

Mirza now spends a few minutes googling some Drina images. He opens a new message and photo from his father: Adem and a woman at an outdoor café table. This is the girlfriend who Adem says isn't. Kristina tends to spit venom when she hears the girlfriend's name. Emina is younger, and a dish — made up like a Belgrade pop diva. Looking at the photo, Mirza admires her profile for a moment, noting his father's happy grin. Then he emails Teo, then his girlfriend Jen. It's been on and off with Jen lately, but it seems she may be willing to see him again. He opens mail from his friend Kemo. They've known each other since they were toddlers. Kemo still lives in Sarajevo, but he spent a summer in Toronto a few years ago. The note brings news that the CD shop on Ferhadija has closed and he's out of work. There is an attached map of Bosnia in stark green and red, the colours separated by the meandering internal border dividing Muslim-Croat Federation from Serbian Republic. It's a joke map. Mirza has already seen it on the Web. The two entities have been renamed *Lažan* and *Beskoristan*: *Bogus* and *Useless*. Coming from Kemo, even as a joke, it seems out of character — as if something more than a job loss is going on.

3

I'm not surprised that Kristina wanted out. Thirteen years later, our father is still the war's visible wound. This thought seems tangled up in the dry clematis vine filling my vision. Sun beats on my head. I'm at the end of my garden and my tether, as far as I can go without getting caught in shrubs and trellises. I become aware of the book in my hand, aware that next to my chair in the living room is a fresh cup of coffee with me no longer beside it in the cool, dry air, settled in the merciful quiet. The voice came. My father, poised in the kitchen over his lunchtime *burek*, in the grip of a meander through memory, a scrap of meaty pastry waiting on his fork. And meanwhile his lips busy with old pleasures or traumas — a swim in the river, a butchered pig, a schoolyard fight, a bombardment, anything.

My father: once a fully convincing professor of history, whose round Hampshire vowels and precise consonants had made him seem English even to some English — until his name, Pero Banjac, was spoken. In Southampton we always pronounced our name as the English did: "*Ban-jack*." Properly, it's closer to "*Ban-yats*." Each summer, on our seaside holidays in Croatia, my sister and I relearned that "*Banjack*" was nonsense.

I observe clusters of tiny black insects on the creeping vine climbing through the dead clematis. For a moment I'm mesmerized by the tight, seething masses, by how aptly they might fuel the misery I will sensibly not succumb to. Almost two weeks of restorative peace — the longest yet — and now the relapse. I simply have to absent myself from my father. Get my nephew in to help rearrange the place, move the books back upstairs, the big chair, the modem maybe? — but Mirza will know. Start using the old study again, get in some more home care, surrender the first floor to Pero. It's either that or continue this pattern of hopeless interjections leading to pointless, crazy-making dialogue.

My eyes focus on the filigree of a dry seed pod. Grief (which I'm beyond, surely — Lyle dead thirteen years now) is ordinary. A fatal car/pedestrian collision resulting in portions of brain spilled onto the upholstery of a Subaru Outback is as plain a catastrophe as a decent tomato with mayonnaise is a plain pleasure. My habit — or when habit fails, my goal — is detachment. Everything is simply what it is. Nothing is surprising. I deliver glib interior lectures to myself on this topic. Ultimately, it all blurs together, the continuous negotiation with days and hours, substandard tomatoes and sucking insects and demented dads. And the dead, all the dead and lamented who abandon the doomed.

As the years of after-Lyle piled up I relearned how to accept everyday pleasures. How to enjoy a tomato, and equally how not to enjoy it, how to care just enough but not too much, if its uncanny perfection of form and colour had the flavour and texture of wet rubber. There are two words for *tomato* in my blood tongue. My father always made the same joke about it. Both *rajčica* and *paradajz*, he rightly said, had heaven in them — exactly what you expect from a proper tomato! Pero trotted out this phonetic bauble all through my childhood. It took me months, after Lyle died, to deny the impulse to pick up a plate of flavourless sliced tomato and pitch it at the kitchen wall. Even now, in my kitchen right next to my father, there is still the dented plaster above the souvenir needlepoint from Sarajevo, still a faint red stain across the hovering Olympic rings and dusty snow-capped mountains.

I move back along the path to a weathered garden chair draped with a pair of men's white briefs. I remove the damp shorts and spread them in the sun on the patio table. I sit in the shade with my book and consider the cover image dully visible through scuffed public library plastic: a stone wall embedded with skulls. I know of this novel. *The*

Excavations made an international literary splash in the 1990s when the world was still interested in the Yugoslavian convulsion. When Pero was moved into my house from Kristina's, the original Serbian edition of the book came along with him, part of a general message from my sister that I ought to take more interest in my ancestry.

As a child, I virtually ignored anything Yugoslav on the family bookshelves. It was not quite as easy to ignore the stories — scraps of reminiscence really — about my parents' wartime years. The events of the 1940s seemed as distant and irrelevant as the old black-and-white war footage on the BBC. Occasionally they made my sister and me sit with them and watch the documentaries. Televison was meant to tell us what they couldn't.

Then one summer in Makarska my sister fell for a Bosnian. To my parents' chagrin, she abandoned her barely begun university studies and left England behind to embrace the homeland — then eventually to see first-hand what it descended to. I had the good luck (almost inevitable, really) to fall for an Englishman. Kristina may somewhat resent, inwardly, the scot-free life I've made in Canada. Not that any life is scot-free, really.

From the shadowed skulls I look up to the garden's modest panorama: Lyle's garden, since entrusted to me. It's still lovely. Yes. Calming. Less manicured, but that's the difference between me and Lyle and always was. He stood right there. *There.* I stretch now and reach my hand into the spot, the earth co-ordinates that once held Lyle on summer evenings. His pre-dinner vodka on the table, always on a coaster to protect the wood though the same wood got soaked at every rainstorm. Lyle stood rather than sat, because every few minutes he would take a wander into the garden, pluck a faded bloom, adjust a frond, nip a stray shoot, then return to the base camp for vodka and contented surveillance.

I'm looking at the sky now, a little trick for pooling the lachrymal spill. Maple leaves flutter at the deep blue. Rose petal scent comes on the breeze. I could pull out that clematis, put in something less fussy, maybe in the fall.

We went to the ancestral city with my parents. At that point, Lyle and I had been together about six years. It was the first time the four of us holidayed together. It seemed to establish that Lyle was a family member — all completely unspoken, naturally. This was the year of the Sarajevo Olympics. Pero and Mara stayed with Kristina and Adem and little Mirza in their flat in Kovači, just above the Turkish market. My parents visited old haunts and looked up old friends. For me and Lyle, of course, there was nothing to revisit. My one previous encounter with Sarajevo had been a few days with family when I was twelve.

I don't know what impulse made me think that live ski-jumping and bobsledding would be thrilling. We decided sports was more tolerable on TV, where fans waved their national flags at a distance. Lyle and I watched most of the games sitting in our room at the Holiday Inn, its recycled air smelling of new paint and carpet fibre. We might almost have been in Calgary or Saskatoon, sitting in identical mustard-yellow wing chairs, except that if we stood at the window, we could see stone minarets clustered beyond the apartment blocks. Lyle was not terribly happy. Almost anywhere Lyle went for a holiday, he indulged a small residue of Englishness that found the amenities wanting. We'd both been that way during our first months in Canada. But one adjusts. What if we'd stayed in England? Lyle might have landed the job at the Royal London Hospital. In any case, he would not have been crossing Carlton Street in the rain on Friday July 28th, 1995.

Now the back door opens, and silence gives way to my father's energetic Serbian: the story of the German officer, grinning executioner of Partisan heroes. Pero hovers in the doorway, pointing his fork at the filthy Krauts. I have heard it a hundred times, maybe more — every inevitable word triggered by the scrap of metal resting in his brain, erasing family and children and forty years of British life, narrowing his past to an endless loop of things that happened long before I was born. This is why Kristina has thrust the skull-adorned book upon me. As if contemplating bones from a two-hundred-year-old battlefield might explain the origins of the shell that fell in Kovači that morning.

4

My nephew touches his dozing grandfather's shoulder.

"*Deda*, it's dinnertime."

Pero's eyes open wide: "Where is Mićo? The trucks are here."

"There's no Mićo, *Deda*. It's me, Mirza."

"Mirza."

"Uncle made burgers. We're going to eat. Don't worry about trucks."

We dine in the house, avoiding the thick heat outside. As Mirza and I chew our juicy burgers, Pero forks apart his well-done one. I've heaped raw onion beside his meat and put the bun on the side. Between swallows, Pero speaks in the language of his youth.

"I went in and told them I'm ready to fight, I want to register. Rajko laughed in my face. Just two years older, but now he's a big soldier man. Only a month after my father died in action, a loyal Partisan, and they act like I'm a joke. No one saw me cry except my own mother, not ever. Yoy! What a day that was." (Here Pero stares deep into Mirza, as if the past is visible behind his grandson's ribs.)

"I would not go home. I stood there and I sang Communist songs. They start to swat me and pull my ears. They drag me out the door, around the back. There's a pump shed. They tie me up in there. The pump, the engine, is going full out. The noise! The stink! They come with a bucket of slops and they dump it over my head. Rajko says to me, 'You know why, little man.' He says, 'You haven't your real balls yet.' He says, 'We can't be wiping your nose for you. We have a war to win.' I said, 'Fuck you. Fuck you, cunt pussies and your mothers. I can fight. I can fight!'"

"*Deda* —"

"So they got one less soldier for Tito. Idiots."

Pero swallows a mouthful and looks at Mirza. "When is Mićo coming?"

"Not today. Finish your burger. And take your meds, okay?"

Mirza slides the med cup a little closer to my father's plate, and Pero eyes it sceptically.

Before dinner Mirza helped me move my reading chair back up to the study. We carted up a few boxes of books. He never balks at helping me with this sort of thing. I won't let him shovel snow or do garden work. At not-quite-fifty, I'm far from incapacitated, though Kristina keeps offering Mirza for the heavier work. Elder care is the primary need. Mirza has even been willing to sit with Pero on the rare weeks we go past the home-care allotment.

We do the washing up and join Pero in the living room. He's quietly snoring on the sofa, hands clasped across his chest. We sit a few moments listening to his fluting whistle.

Mirza says, "Did I tell you I might be moving out? She's thinking of selling the house."

"I heard. It'll be good for you."

"Thing is, I don't have a job."

"Have you looked?"

"Not really, not recently."

"Well, might be an idea. You're how old now?"

"Twenty-five."

"Do you think you should have a job? Artists do, sometimes. I haven't said it, Mirza, but you've pretty much been coasting for a few years. I don't mean your work, your sculpture and so on, but just financially — and more or less by your mother's good graces."

We watch each other. Mirza has a slightly defiant look.

"I'm working on a project. I have some grant money."

"You do? Well, good. I mean congratulations."

"Eighteen thousand."

"Oh. That's a chunk. Does your mother know?"

"No. It's for the installation: materials and research.

There's interest in my work from MOCCA."

"Mocha?"

"The new contemporary art museum, on Queen West. My agent said she can get me in there. They're showcasing new artists in October — you know, hot young things. And I've got use of a studio."

"Good heavens. This sounds grand. Why didn't you say?"

"It's not settled. Except the grant money. I heard last week."

"You know, if your mother does boot you out, you might stay here if you like. Save you spending your grant on rent."

"Only if she boots me?"

"Not only. Regardless. You're welcome here. You'd have your old room and bath. I won't expect extra *Deda* care, or not much. And I won't mother you, make you eat more vegetables."

"I like vegetables."

"I realize you may have other offers — perhaps more enticing than moving back in with your grandpa."

"Teo thinks we should get an apartment."

"I see. Does he like vegetables too?"

"He lives on red meat and potatoes."

"Does *he* have a job?"

"Freelance. He does illustrations."

Pero shifts, and his eyes open: "Where is Mićo? Is he hurt?"

"Mićo is okay, *Deda*," says Mirza. "Go back to sleep."

Pero closes his eyes. Within minutes he is snoring again.

I get off the streetcar and backtrack along King to the massive Victorian factory building filled with studios and lofts. An elevator wheezes me to the fourth floor, where I find Mirza's door and knock, to no response. I crack open the door and announce myself, then walk in. The cool air is vaguely acrid: a burnt plastic smell. I'm in a narrow, high-ceilinged white room. Scattered in front of arched windows are eight or ten life-size human figures. On a broad table I can see Mirza's backpack among a clutter of objects: an electric chainsaw, power drill, a machete, a blowtorch, plastic jugs of liquid, all crowding a computer monitor showing an image of a cemetery and the words *SREBRENIČKE MAJKE*. I look at the figures under the windows: naked clothing store dummies, male and female. They've been altered, damaged. The door opens behind me.

"Uncle."

"I walked in. I hope you don't mind."

"I asked you, didn't I?"

I move closer to the mannequins. Some have been heavily abused: ears hacked off, skulls broken into, faces disfigured. Eyes are burned out. There are wounds in torsos, what look like bullet holes. The breasts of a female have been burned black and crusted with reddish clots. A male's abdomen is just a mangled hole.

"This is early. They need more detailed work, layers, and clothes of course, scraps of clothing, and hair, and dirt, mud."

I glance at the computer screen. "Srebrenica."

"No. It's not site-specific. Installed, they'll be at a cocktail party but with their nice clothes filthy and in complete ruins so they're half naked. They'll have drinks. Two of the males will be waiters, with finger food on trays."

I'm examining a bullet hole. "How did you — ?"

"I shot them. Out in the woods near your cottage. I borrowed a gun. I might actually go back and drag some of them behind the car up there, on the gravel. I mean late at night."

"That would be wise."

"It's how you spin it. First, no actual massacre reference. When people enter the gallery, they get an invitation card."

Mirza moves to his computer. Text comes up:

*The Office of the High Investigator
and the
International Coalition for Peace
request your presence at a reception in
The Atrium
honouring the
Research and Identification Commission
upon the successful completion of forensic
excavation and analysis
in the Southeast Exhumation Quadrant of the
Republic.
Wine and canapes will be served.*

"Of course, we'll have real wine and food at the opening."

"Will they have an appetite?"

Mirza smiles. I am not smiling, but I'm not shocked, exactly. I'm wondering what shift in Mirza's psyche might have led to this.

"Does your mother know?"

"She hates the whole concept."

"Your father?"

"He'll probably never see it. He wants me to come to Bosnia. He's got this pyramid thing going."

"Pyramid."

"Bosnian Pyramids. He's got a construction deal for the reception centre in Visoko. I think I'll go. I can stay in the apartment. I need to do some reconnecting, and research. Not about pyramids."

"That's a relief."

"I'll have to, you know, drive a truck for him or something."

"When were you there last?"

"Before we left."

"That was — ten years ago."

"Twelve."

5

They are human but not real. You get inside under the cool plastic skin, and the flesh is made of inert composite stuff. Harming them is a game, like what kids do to exercise their pointless aggression. Mirza does feel something like a bad little boy, chopping away at a skull or pouring acid into an eye socket. But it doesn't mean he doubts the project. If it offends, that's good, even the main point. He is offended by his memories. For twelve years they've been pictures that visit him, sometimes at random or sometimes because of a loud noise in the street. They wake him up out of dreams. He can usually just shove them back in their box, but this project has turned out to be an extended opening of the box.

Now suddenly he is offended. The hole in his grandfather's head. The blood pooled on the kitchen floor. When the shelling stopped, they rushed *Deda* to Koševo Hospital, and Mirza was left alone with the mess. They told him to stay in the vestibule, but they were gone for so long. He began to wipe up the dark puddles and sticky footprints with dish towels. It only spread the blood and its smell, and it dried on the tiles in red-brown smears. Adem came home and took over, mopping the floor with the old dishwater they saved in a bucket. Then Kristina came and stuffed the bloody towels into the woodstove and wept, sobbing in his ear and hugging the breath out of him.

The project raises memories in surprising detail. The upside is the creative rush, the steady progress of what, in his mind, he has taken to calling *the excavations*, a title he saw on his grandfather's bookshelf. He can just let his intuition guide him. No chance of real blood appearing, no screams, no mother's tears. The blood is painted on, smeared off, painted or splashed on again, trying to get it right. The painted blood is bright red for some figures, as if recently tortured or shot. For the exhumed, he needs clotted effects, some achieved with actual blood he gets from a butcher in Greektown.

Now that Teo knows about the grant money, he is asking questions. Mirza deflects them for a while, but then he's coerced into saying more, just enough to make him feel he's left a completely wrong impression. He invites his friend to the studio. When Teo walks in, he seems kind of dumbstruck. He basically says, "Yeah, interesting." He stares at the images of gravestones and exhumation sites on Mirza's computer. Then he wants to go for beer. They head to a Parkdale dive and drink till past midnight, talking about peripheral stuff. Finally, Teo begins to ask some questions, but not about the work. He says, "Why do you want to go back there, back to that shit?" And so Mirza tells him he actually *is* going back, to Sarajevo, for real, and soon. Teo stares at him.

"Why would you do that?"

"The project. Research. I'll stay with my father."

"What research?"

"It's obvious."

"Srebrenica?"

"Partly."

"Fuck. It's a graveyard."

"So we should just forget about it?"

"Yeah. You live here now."

"I'm not here sometimes. I can't help it."

"So you have to fix that."

"That's what I'm doing."

"What you're doing is wallowing. I think it might even be kind of sick."

Their eyes stay glued on each other. Teo is right, in a way, but it's the old trap.

"It's *about* sick."

"Sick with people, sick with dummies, whatever, it's the same sick. Fuck. What are you thinking, Mickey?"

Mirza stares into his beer glass.

"I call you Teo." He looks up. "That's your name. So you can call me Mirza. I think we should retire Mickey, okay?"

Teo stares at him with his mouth open.

"You know," Mirza says, "there's a reason you dropped out in third year."

"Really. What's that?"

"Same reason we're having this conversation. Your work is divorced from your experience."

"And what is my work?"

"Well what is it? Are you still painting? I mean, selling stuff to magazines is good, but —"

Teo gets out of his chair. He stands a moment, just staring into the air, then turns and strides toward the washrooms. When he returns, he goes to pay for his beer at the bar and then comes back to the table. He leans on his hands with his face level with Mirza's.

"You should talk to someone. Seriously."

"I'm talking to you."

Teo is already heading for the door.

Biking home brings some clarity. The bike is part of him, the handlebars and wheels extensions of his body, a single machine that's all motion yet keeps him firm inside himself. Cars and people and buildings slide by. He simply had to say what he had to say. Finally he said it, letting it out. He's finished with pretending that the past has somehow disappeared. It's actually sad about Teo — his refusal to face what's in him, to feed it into creation, make it fuel his work.

Going up Broadview he makes a decision that's barely conscious. Just past the streetcar loop at Danforth he veers right and moments later is bumping over the sidewalk and up the narrow path beside his uncle's house. He locks the bike and stands breathing. TV light flickers in the neighbour's house, but Alex's windows are dark. He lets himself in at the back door.

Alex's fridge offers the remains of a roast chicken. He eats standing up, pulling apart the bones with his hands, sucking off the last morsels. He finds soft rye bread and makes a mayo and hot mustard sandwich and eats it in a rapture. Then the pressing thought of a cold glass of milk. As he pours the milk, his uncle comes into the kitchen in his terry bathrobe. Mirza takes a long sip, watching Alex watch him.

"You didn't wake me. I was reading."

Mirza drinks half the milk and wipes his mouth. "I was starved. Kind of had beer for dinner. Teo came by the studio."

"Do you want to stay?"

"Okay, thanks."

"Couch all right?"

Mirza belches. "Sure." He blurts, "Teo hates

the project too."

"I didn't say I hated it. What happened? Did you argue?"

"Sort of. He's got more shit to deal with, I guess."

"Shit meaning ..."

"Well — um, do you mind if I have a drink?"

"Of course not. I'll join you. Come and sit."

His uncle moves ahead of him into the living room, turning on lights. He pours and hands Mirza the Scotch, and the way he settles into his chair and looks right at Mirza's face seems to say he is ready to grapple.

"I'm okay. It's actually Teo who's not okay."

"What did Teo say?"

"He said it's sick. The concept itself is sick."

"Then he and I don't agree."

"Thank you."

"You're recognizing, demonstrating, well, a pathology. War as a global pathology."

"Right."

"His approach may be different."

"Totally. He doesn't approach it."

"I'll admit, the work distresses me a little. Just because it's you and, as you said, it also disturbs your mother."

"What am I supposed to do?"

"I don't know."

"She's not involved in my work. It's not her

business."

"Another reason you should move out, perhaps."

"Anyway, I'll be gone for most of the summer." Mirza stares into the amber liquid in his glass. "I'm going to Srebrenica." He can feel his uncle's assessing silence.

"What will you do there?"

"Absorb it. Talk to people, take pictures. Talk in Bosnian." He takes a sip of the Scotch. He's alert now. He feels exactly drunk enough. "I need to make it present again. I mean the whole place. Sarajevo, the neighbourhood. People. You know? Instead of these old pictures in my mind." His uncle simply watches him. "I was talking to Kemo. Guy in Sarajevo I've known since I was four. He was here two summers ago."

"I remember."

"His brother was in the army. He went missing, just, like, a month or two before the war ended. They knew when and where, but they never found him. He was, I don't know, maybe nineteen or twenty. I remember him. Halid. So someone a year ago is clearing out junk behind a factory, old oil barrels, and they open one up and there's a guy in there, remains, and they get sent for DNA and they figure out it's Halid. The family got the ID it was him just last week. I heard from Kemo. He was tortured; they could tell from the bones. You know what they did to him?"

"Don't tell me. So, you'll go there and, what? It seems, I don't know — a little out of left field."

"Maybe you don't understand."

"I understand you're affected by your friend's —"

"Affected." Mirza grins. He feels warm inside. He is warmly and agreeably offended. His uncle really hasn't a clue what this means to him. "You sound like Teo."

"Maybe we just want you to stay the Mirza we know."

"Who is that? I mean, fuck ..." He rolls his head around.

"Perhaps you've had enough to drink, also."

"Oh, well, thanks for the info." He is still softly grinning. He gets up and goes to the bottle and pours himself a little more. He watches Alex's face over the rim as he takes a sip. Then he tips it all back into his mouth and swallows. It burns its way down. He opens his mouth and makes Bosnian come out. "*Spava mi se.*" He needs to sleep.

Alex makes up the couch in the TV room.

Mirza pulls off his clothes and stands in his underwear as his uncle tucks corners and plumps pillows. Alex quickly moves past him to the door.

"You're all set?"

Mirza swings his torso around. "Yeah."

"Okay. *Laku noć.*"

"*A tibi.*"

Alex pulls the door gently shut.

Mirza lies down. Just drunk enough. No spins, not real ones, only a slight and pleasing sideways drift that he can arrest and reset before he slides off again. He wakes out of a deep sleep and goes to pee. Then dreams. Riding his bike. He falls with a bump. Then Kemo in an oil barrel, compressed. Mirza pulls him out, and he is okay. But there are more barrels they have to check, somewhere along a muddy road. They find a dead soldier in a barnyard. His head is like a smashed melon with a hairy green rind. A chicken is pecking at the pink brain.

Mirza wakes up, his forehead and chest damp with sweat. There is grey light outside the window. This soldier and chicken come back now and then in his dreams. They were in a news photo he saw when he was a child. He actually clipped it from the paper and saved it, secretly, until one day in a fit of disgust he burned it in the stove. The image obsessed and appalled him, to see this evidence, that a man's brain, his mind, his self, could be ...

He dozes. When he comes to again, there is bright sunlight in the room. His dick is semi-hard. He touches it lightly and scans the room for a box of tissues. He's thinking about the time with Jen at her cottage, on the old couch in the breezeway, her butt up in the air and he on his knees behind, slipping in and out of her and watching her parents down at the dock, just getting out of the boat, and he kept humping her knowing they couldn't see through the screens as they came up the hill. Risk was the entire turn-on. Jen herself, especially lately, he can take or leave. He gets up and goes to the bathroom for some tissue, but by then he's getting soft. He pees and thinks he'll just give in to the scent of coffee and toast drifting up from the kitchen. His uncle will likely be heading off to his library job.

Mirza finds eggs in the fridge. A fresh pot of coffee is dripping. Before leaving the house, Alex comes and pauses at the kitchen door.

"How are you feeling?"

"Fine. Really."

"*Deda* is getting dressed. Homecare comes at ten. Just please make sure to lock the gate if you go out the back way."

"Sure. Sorry I came by so late."

"No need for sorry. I'm glad we talked."

Mirza pours a mug of coffee and fries himself three eggs, sliding them onto buttered toast. He has the strange hangover clarity again, enhanced by his uncle's strong brew. He sits and eats his breakfast, looking out at the garden: the garden that is Lyle's. Lyle's achievement, Lyle's memorial. Mirza remembers his mother crying about the news from Toronto, a car accident. It was the last summer of the war. They sat in the July swelter listening to the snipers and eating their rice and beans. "And we're still here," she said, and they all stared at their thoughts, but there wasn't any way to compute it.

His uncle has this different, less complicated sadness. He has the ordinary progress of a life, from England to Toronto, arriving at this house and these white roses on the trellis. Morning sun on the creamy petals and dark leaves. Maybe someday Mirza can have this. Maybe someone to love and lose, only by ordinary good or bad luck. He'll have a house and that quiet pleasure he's noticed in older people with their gardens. He'll have a demented old father, and mother too, and some roses like these ones.

His uncle is worried about him. Everyone has concerns about Mirza. He maybe should not have mentioned the bones in the barrel, the torture. He'd been aware of the effect of his words on Alex. He was only thinking out loud, in a way he simply cannot do with his mother — and maybe not with his uncle either. He slowly chews and swallows his eggs. On the patio, his grandfather's baggy underpants are draped over the usual chair in the usual way. He can hear Pero moving around upstairs now.

6

In the time just before the siege, Pero went out on Saturdays with his grandson. They gawked at the shop windows, stopped at Markale market for pastries, maybe saw a film at the Imperial. He sought out old friends in the cafés so he could show Mirza off. It was a way for him to reconnect with his city and family both, making it feel all of a piece, as if the years in England had been an interruption in the natural flow. They usually passed by the Serbian cathedral, just as they did on the day of the shootings.

There was a small crowd outside the church, and on the steps going in, a wedding party. The sound of shots and screams put Pero back fifty years, as if German soldiers were still ruling the streets. He clamped Mirza by the arm and ran, the boy lagging and bleating at him, until they were safely away in a side street. They stood there, Pero bent double, his heart jumping like a rabbit. Mirza was whining, clutching his chafed wrist. He snapped at the boy.

"Stop your nonsense. I just saved your skin."

Mirza looked up at him, the dark eyes with tears forming. The boy wiped his face with a quick backhand and levelled his gaze at a shop window opposite. They stared at racks of ladies' dress shoes. A hand appeared in the window and chose a pair from the display, as if the day was like any other.

When Pero had recovered his breath, they walked back through Vase Miskina. Mirza was silent, keeping pace, his hand in Pero's. As they went through Baščaršija, Pero saw Šaban in his usual *kafana* window, and he stopped in to report what they'd witnessed. The TV over the bar was tuned to a football game. Šaban listened to him indifferently and surmised the gunman might have been a spurned lover.

At the apartment, Adem and Kristina were oblivious. Pero thought they might have just finished making love. They had that jaunty, evasive look about them. In two months with them he'd discerned the patterns. He told them about the shooting as he went to turn on the television. He switched channels, found a brief report: two men shot outside the Serbian cathedral. Then back to the usual political nonsense.

Later, the shooting was at the top of the evening news. A reporter in the forecourt of the church, blood on the stone steps behind him, a shot of weeping bridesmaids with makeup-streaked faces. The groom's father had been killed, the priest injured. It seemed the killers were known. They watched the screen in silence. Two men from the wedding party were interviewed, their voices forced-casual, faces like stone. Pero knew the look. It was about biding time. The score eventually would be evened. A third man told the camera, "Clear as me here in front of you, Ćelo and his gang. They got out of the car and began firing." He sucked on his cigarette, and his eyes shifted as if seeing all that would come of it. "He's laughing now."

Adem spoke to the television.

"Fucking Ćelo. What are you doing?"

Kristina said quietly, with an edge of sarcasm, "He's a murderer. The whole city knows it."

Adem ignored her and held his eyes on the screen. "Why would he do it? It's bullshit. It's a mistaken identity."

"I don't want to see him again."

"See him? You never see him."

"No more. Break off with him. I don't care if he's your fourth or fifteenth or whatever cousin."

Adem turned up the volume. Someone was saying it was not Ćelo's car, then he was drowned out by mocking voices. A large man, his shoulders straining the fabric of his suit, took hold of the interviewer's microphone. "Let me say..." His paw engulfed the reporter's. "Ćelo's car is not guilty. No one saw his car. The car is innocent. Maybe he took his mother's car. Ma! I need to shoot some

Serbs today!" Men in the crowd began shouting.

Adem turned off the TV. Pero got out of his chair and turned it on again.

"If you don't object? We were there. I would like to see the news."

"I'm sorry. Watch it, yes. But it's bullshit. Excuse me, that's what I think."

Kristina said, "What did you see, *Tata*?"

"Nothing. We heard the shots and ran."

Adem left the room. He came back putting on his jacket. He said to Kristina, "Should I break off with Serb crooks too? I have to swim in this water. That's it. If we want an income, yes? It's business, Krista." He left the apartment.

Pero had heard from his café circle that Ćelo was mafia. It was news to him that Adem had dealings with the man. Shooting a wedding guest in broad daylight seemed absurdly brazen. Of course, he wanted the witnesses, the media show. It was a declaration. Pero observed Mirza staring at the TV screen.

"Shall we watch some football, Mirza?"

"It's Australian."

"Better than none."

Mirza turned to his mother. "Why is Ćelo shooting Serbs?"

"He's bad man, that's all, a criminal."

"Is *Tata* his friend?"

"Business, Mirza. Not a friend."

"Why did he shoot the priest?"

"Maybe they were his enemies."

"But you are Serb too."

Kristina stared at her son. "I'm what? I'm Serb? Who told you this?"

"My teacher."

"Who is she to say I'm Serb? She can't say that."

"She told us about our names. She said Kristina is Serb. Mirza is Muslim. Tata's name is Muslim too. I already knew from Kemo."

"You are not Muslim, darling. Your teacher doesn't know. Have you ever gone to a mosque? Does your father go? Never mind what you're hearing at school. Who is this teacher?"

"Mrs. Suljić. She's Muslim too."

"Mirza, Mirza —"

Kristina glanced round the room, and her eyes locked briefly onto Pero's. She sat opposite Mirza and took both of his hands in hers.

"Listen to me. This was not a lesson. This was the teacher's politics. She is wrong. We are a family. Not one thing or another thing. Who is she to teach this? What happened to Miss Gajić?"

"She went to Banja Luka."

Kristina looked up at Pero: the hunted look again. She let go of Mirza's hands and sat staring into space.

Pero said, "His teacher is right. We are Serbs."

"Don't say it."

"It has been said."

"I won't… I will not —" She stared hard at him. "Who is 'we'? Who do you mean?"

"You and me, Krista, who else?"

"We are a family. Me and Adem and Mirza and you. We are a Yugoslav and a British family."

Pero remembered her like this as a teenager, when she announced that she would marry Adem and live with him in Sarajevo. She defied him with a clarity that shocked him but also made him proud. It had secretly gratified him that she would be back in Bosnia, in his hometown, in what had become the most Yugoslav of cities.

"You might phone the school."

"I will. The principal. He's a Yugoslav too."

"People change."

"Not us."

Later in the evening, Pero switched on an old war drama. Adem was still out. Krista and Mirza went to bed, and Pero was left alone with the flickering black and white images: intrepid Partisan soldiers fighting Germans and Italians. For a while he succumbed to the uncomplicated heroics.

As he prepared a bedtime mug of tea, he heard Adem come in, then the renewed sound of the television. He came out of the kitchen. On the screen, civic leaders were sparring in a news studio. He joined his son-in-law on the couch. A ripe brandy scent rolled off of Adem. In silence they watched the petulant skirmishes.

Adem turned to him: "Who would you shoot first? Hey? Come on. I'm serious." He swivelled his head back to the screen, watching it with a tight smile.

7

Something about the church shootings tipped Pero into a bout of nostalgia. He needed to counter the senselessness of the attack. He found himself opening old photo albums and a box of letters from the war years. He had once tried reading some of these letters to Aleksandar and Kristina as children, but they'd been indifferent. Now, here in the Kovači apartment with his young grandson, it seemed time to try again. Mirza should be made to know that war could be honourable, unlike these stupid battles between street thugs.

Maybe they would have to leave Bosnia now that lines were being drawn again and guns brandished, but the boy should know that in Partisan days there was, there truly was, a brotherhood of honour, of collective responsibility. Pero felt the spirit of this in his bones again when he read his father's letters. History had its practical and moral uses, one of them to show children that a just war might even inspire the birth of a nation.

When Adem and Kristina were out one day,

Pero sat himself at the kitchen table with his bundle of letters while Mirza was eating. With a subtle show of reverence, he untied the bundle and silently began to read, as if so completely absorbed that he had forgotten Mirza's presence. Occasionally he released soft exclamations of admiration. Mirza gave him scant attention. He was more interested in his sandwich. Pero looked at him.

"Did you know that your great-grandfather knew Comrade Tito?"

"Who is my great-grandfather?"

"Not is. Was. He was my father. He died fighting for Yugoslavia. Do you sing songs for Tito in school?"

Mirza spoke through a mouthful. "No. They stopped."

"That's a shame. When did they stop?"

"When I was little."

"You are not little now?"

The songs were passé. Pero knew it. They were a small footnote to history lessons. Well, here was a better history lesson: "Your great-grandfather was a Partisan fighter. He believed that all people could live in one nation of brotherhood. That was Tito's great hope. And he did it. He made Yugoslavia into one big commune."

"I know that, *Deda*."

"All right, you know. But you don't know what is in these letters. This one, for instance, is from

Milovan Djilas, a man who was a personal comrade to Tito, a commander."

"I know that."

"Yes, good, and after the war this Djilas wrote books about the Partisan struggle. He also wrote this letter to your great-grandfather, Sveto Banjac. Listen. It's not long. I want you to learn something besides the nonsense you get on television."

Pero began reading, pressing on through the feeling that he was proving himself just one more faded *nostalgnik* — less a realist than the boy was, in fact. He tried to infuse the words with drama.

Comrade Sveto,

I hope this reaches you before the usual hearsay. No matter the rumours, we claimed a rousing victory at Velje Brdo against the Chetniks. We are now stationed with the Piperi clan, attempting to save them from Italian and Albanian brutalities. Coming down at dusk from Trijebač to the village, we passed empty shells of houses and a woman weeping by the side of the road. In her hands was a photograph in a broken frame. I caught a glimpse of a young man in uniform beneath the cracked glass. In the dying rays of the sun, the armed peasants walked quietly past her. I passed by like the rest, thinking that war was war, and that the lesson was always clear: each and every death must be made to have meaning. The meaning is found daily in our struggle to build a future apart from these deaths, to fight with courage and discipline and honour and, finally, to wrest a lasting peace and a united Yugoslav state from the jaws of Fascism and enmity.

Before dawn yesterday we got to a plateau overlooking the Zeta where we awaited sunrise. In the green valley, the even greener Italian soldiers approached the stone huts, and smoke began to pour out of them. Beside me, as the daylight came up, Blažo saw that his own house was already afire. Days before, his mother and wife and children had fled into the hills. Peasants from the river hamlets were now on the road beside us with their animals and children and belongings. They trudged by as Blažo and I watched them in silence. Down among the burning houses there was still shooting — no doubt at the chickens.

Along came a peasant staggering under the weight of a cannon wheel.

He sat down near us to rest, and I said to him, "What is that for?"

He replied: "Well, it may come in handy." I asked him calmly what use a single cannon wheel might be to him. He repeated that it just might come in handy someday.

Suddenly I was incensed: "Don't you have anything better to do than to lug that thing up a mountain?" I took the wheel and dragged it to the edge and sent it spinning down the precipice. We watched it crash through the trees and vanish. "There," I said. "You will find it there after the war."

Yours in struggle,
Djido

Pero carefully folded the letter. Mirza had finished his sandwich.

"Why did they shoot the chickens?"

"For food of course. And perhaps out of spite. But do you understand what Djilas meant, by the story of the cannon wheel?"

"It was stolen."

"Possibly, but the point is that the peasant had more important responsibilities. There was a struggle going on to defend his way of life, his whole world. He could have joined with the fighters like Djilas."

"Maybe he did."

"Yes. Maybe he did. Many joined up. It's why

the Communists finally won. They had an inspiring vision, for a better world, a world of equality for all."

"*Deda*, everyone says the Communists are finished."

"They are. You're right. But you should know something. My old friends from when I was just a lad in the Brigades, they still know people in the army, in the People's Army of Yugoslavia, which is not finished. It's up in the hills around Sarajevo at this very moment, getting ready to stop this idiotic farce, these opportunists and neo-Chetniks and Islamists. This will all be over in a month. Europe and America will support us, and Bosnia will be a free nation."

Kristina arrived home, bearing a loaf of bread and a few tins of meat and the news that Adem had gone for manoeuvres and would not be home for three days. She had not gone to her neighbourhood meeting. Instead, she'd spent over two hours in a queue for food. She put the items down on the table.

"Do you see this? This is to last us until Friday. Food is now a criminal enterprise."

"I'll go tomorrow to the bank. We'll pay whatever's needed."

"Go now."

"All right. I'll just have a bite first."

"Now, *Tata*. Now."

Pero's eyes met hers. He got out of his chair and fetched his wallet and coat and left the apartment.

He hadn't been out in two or three days. The queues in the street seemed longer. He walked to the bank near the Catholic church, where he could access funds from his British account. He came away about three hours later with one hundred deutschmarks, the allowed limit, pushing his way through people who'd been shut out.

8

For years, I spoke with Kristina only at holiday time. That changed abruptly. One morning, Lyle came into the bathroom.

"Alex. Your sister."

"My sister?"

"On the phone. From Sarajevo."

I took the phone, wiping shave cream from my face.

"Krista, what's up?"

"Sorry, it's early there."

"No, no, we're up. We've been thinking of you. With the referendum and everything. Good news."

"I don't know."

"How are you? How is everyone?"

"Well, it's why I'm calling. So much is happening here. We're considering whether we should leave, before things deteriorate any more. Adem would probably stay. There's a lot of pressure, and he wants to do the right thing." I could hear the strain in her voice, the effort at control. "The city is dividing up."

"What do you mean?"

"They have barricades up around the city. They're dividing it by how the neighbourhoods stack up. They're creating almost — front lines. It feels insane, but it's happening."

"Where are you?"

"We're at home. For now. It's possible I'll go away with Mirza and Daddy, to the coast, to Adem's family."

"Without Adem?"

"He feels he'd be running."

"Sounds like running is required."

"We had that discussion. I can't get through to him. He has a gun now, some kind of, I don't know, assault thing. People are arming."

"Oh, Krista."

"I was just beginning to think I understood my country."

"Can you go out, I mean at all, just for food or ...?"

"I don't know. I will have to." Kristina's voice hardened. "Ordinary people didn't do this. It's the bloody politicians, the criminal elites."

"Can't the police — ?"

"The police are choosing sides like everyone else."

"You should go, just go."

"I don't know. If we're not able to come back ... There's a protest tomorrow. There will be thousands.

People don't want this. We're waiting to see if the EC recognizes Bosnia, and the Americans, what they're going to do about it. Everyone says they won't let a war happen."

"They let it happen in Croatia."

"The situation was different. There's just a lot of emotion right now, and distrust, people blaming the Serbs."

"Where does that leave you and Daddy?"

"What?" Kristina seemed surprised. "We're Bosnians. Now more than ever. I mean, this is why we should stay, at least for now. If we get independence, are recognized, the goons can't have their way."

Kristina called a few days later. The barricades were down, but tension seemed to have increased. At the weekend protest, two people had been killed by shots from apartment towers. Adem was organizing a neighbourhood defence unit. Krista's voice on the phone was flat, almost emotionless. "We're sitting it out."

Then, for more than three years, there was almost no phone communication. Letters disappeared or took months to arrive. Memories of my Olympics visit eight years before were set against news reports that gave vague or sometimes disturbingly specific news of where the bombs were falling. The random shell that erased my father's memory did it five days before I heard the news from Kristina, in a few allotted minutes on a UN phone. I learned that my father was in a hospital bed and could not speak or recognize his daughter. Krista said that shells had hit even the hospital that morning.

They survived, applied for refugee status, came to Toronto. For almost four months, my sister, Adem, Pero, and thirteen-year-old Mirza lived in my house. At that point, Lyle had been dead nearly a year. The full house and busy days, the fact of their escape and a fresh beginning, helped me to climb out of grieving that had lost its purpose and settled into a wallow. I took vacation days from the library. I accompanied them to hearings, got them set up with counselling, booked Adem and Mirza into ESL classes, took them apartment-hunting and on streetcar and subway jaunts. We even picnicked once on Hanlan's Point — my impulse to let the gay contingent serve as one more Toronto culture primer.

Our dinners at home ranged from lively to subdued, depending on the outcomes of the day. I learned that ignoring Pero's monologues was the best strategy, either that or using food or TV as an intervention. Kristina insisted on cooking, which revived the flavours of my childhood. A minor sore point was Adem's total aversion to kitchen work. He never touched a pot, made a sandwich, or washed a dish. He did repaint the front porch, and made a professional job of it.

It was a spring and summer of interrupted sleep. I woke to Mirza's night terrors. Footsteps came on the stairs, then the smell of toast wafting up from the kitchen and Kristina's returning steps, bringing the food to Mirza in bed. If I got up to prowl, I might find Adem on the front porch, smoking and waiting for the dawn. Sometimes my father was there too in his pyjamas and robe. They sat there, each silently observing the neighbourhood as if the other wasn't present. Adem had a gift for stifling Pero's monologue impulse. He simply said, a clipped bark, "Shut it."

Adem and Kristina could not agree on an apartment. They fought about this and other things, sometimes first thing in the morning. Once, I came home to overhear Adem protesting to Kristina that he had nothing against gays. He was forcing laughter, trying to make light of it while she spat her fury at him.

I came up with a financing plan to help get them resettled. We found a bungalow on Gamble Avenue, about five minutes away. I took on the mortgage, and we settled on a rent-to-buy agreement. By then, Adem was getting steady construction work. Through a contact at the refugee centre, Kristina got a part-time position at a small publishing house. Mirza was enrolled in school and began meeting other Bosnian kids in the schoolyard, along with children in shades of tan and brown he'd never before encountered.

9

My sister sometimes refers to Mirza's single injury sustained during the siege. After a sponge bath, he'd backed into the oil-drum wood stove they'd rigged up in the apartment kitchen. Mirza's war wound was a large blister on his bum. Adem and Kristina went out into the dangerous streets, probably hundreds of times, simply to obtain the necessities of life, not to mention what Adem faced on the front lines. Yet they are, physically at least, more or less intact. My father stayed off the streets and nonetheless won the shrapnel lottery. Pero is a cypher of what he was. Happily, he doesn't consider himself a cypher. Life engages him. He often has the look of someone intensely occupied by the people and things around him, even if (especially if) they are ghosts.

On Pero's balding head about two inches above the left eye is a hollow lined with scar tissue. Deep beneath it sits the fragment of metal. Surgery was long ago ruled out — too much risk of further damage. Medically, my father is stable, but they estimate that he remembers only about five to seven minutes of the immediate past. His life is being continually erased. Incoming information fills the short loop, then itself gets deleted as more data comes in. The cache of memory seems to be enough for most mundane activities. He can eat, because the disappearing food in front of him is being re-recorded constantly onto the recall loop. Spatial memory seems more reliable. He goes up and down the stairs, finds his way to the various rooms in my house, though it took weeks for the patterns to imprint after he moved in. My father might mistake his nephew for an old school friend, but he never mistakes the front hall for the kitchen. He remembers basic skills learned long ago, such as brushing his teeth. He's fine in the shower as long as someone is there to tell him when to come out.

He recalls his distant past in detail, though always in disjointed patches. He can talk about boyhood and wartime incidents as if they happened yesterday or an hour ago. What he seems not to remember at all are events from roughly 1950 to the present. My father is two people I barely know: the old man who often behaves like something from an absurdist piece of theatre, and the child and teenager in wartime Sarajevo or afterward, rebuilding his country with his gung-ho Brigade pals. It's as if he never became a full adult. The years in England, the husband-and-father years, are missing. Pero similarly has no future. Every plan and anticipation lasts only moments before it disappears.

He can still speak and understand English, though his default setting is always his childhood tongue. He still reads books. What he absorbs is unknown. On the shelf beside the sofa on which he spends his days are perhaps thirty titles, all that remains of his Southampton library. On a lower shelf sits a residue of scholarly and personal papers in cardboard file boxes: reminders of the mind that generated a teaching career, a history of Bosnia, and an unpublished memoir of his wartime childhood. Pero usually sets a book aside after five or ten minutes of attention, but he returns to certain bookmarked passages, reading them over and over as if each time is the first. The typed pages of his unfinished memoir are so fragile from handling that Kristina made photocopies and stored them out of reach.

On Pero's shelf is also the novel with skulls on the cover. These bones are legendary. Tourists still trickle to the old battle site to see them. Even I know this, though I've spent a lifetime indifferent to my heritage. They are the skulls of Serb fighters, killed by Turks who then mortared them into a victory wall. Pero's hardcover copy has the worn look of a personal talisman: its dust jacket held together with tape, its pages smudged from handling. My spotty household Serbian from childhood is useless for interpreting the Cyrillic text, but I've recently obtained an English edition from the Toronto Public Library. It even reproduces, somewhat gauzily, the same skulls on the cover.

I have watched people blunt grief with television, shopping, travel, liquor, anything to make the mind fill with something else or nothing. After Lyle, I did it mainly with books and Scotch whisky, the whisky priced so far beyond my budget that I couldn't overdo it — well, not too often. Yesterday, with a sense of mission and a Macallan, I cracked open my copy of the skull novel.

The Excavations presented me with Istok Nemirić, a guru-philosopher rendered paralyzed during the shelling of a Dalmatian resort hotel. Mute and immobile, he becomes an oracle wired to a computer, through which he dispenses his eccentric thoughts on the universe. The novelist himself, Dragomir Nemirić, had been slightly injured in the 1991 bombing of Dubrovnik. In the book, the paralyzed Nemirić is taken by his desperate family to the Herzegovina shrine of Medjugorje, site of supposed Marian apparitions. After several months in a charmless motel room filled with crucifixes and plastic Virgins, enduring holy water rubbed five times daily into the spot where his neck vertebrae were snapped, Istok finally, by heroic efforts, manages to communicate to his family that he can't stand the place, by which point the war in Bosnia is in full swing.

I'm finding the satirical tone of the book stimulating. My parents were never church-goers. Pero, whose parents were card-carrying Communists, was a staunch non-believer. It pleases me to think that my father, who I grew up thinking of as a committed, even rather dusty academic, somehow came to possess and value such a fanciful and sardonic piece of work.

When I think about angels or Marian visions, I consider them on a par with fairies and space aliens — they all share a random, marginal, inconsequential quality. I put the faith question to rest long ago, but Lyle's death briefly revived it with all its galling absurdities. I still sometimes wake in the night and run internal monologues on the God I don't believe in: if there is a divine creator who sends visions to inspire and heal humankind, why does he skimp so cruelly? Why cure bad backs and an occasional cancer while neglecting to schedule the Virgin for some time with the people of Sarajevo or Srebrenica? Faith seems to give people a licence to be idiots — an uncharitable thought, but I simply can't erase it. A recent TV news item reported a woman in Kentucky who'd seen an image of the Blessed Virgin on a fried pork chop. The woman posted a photo of the miracle chop on the Internet before storing it away in her freezer. I wondered at the time if she had considered eating it. People eat Jesus in church every Sunday — why not eat his mother? These questions are endless.

Lyle was struck by the Subaru Outback while crossing on a green light in a driving rainstorm at the intersection of Church and Carlton Streets. The Subaru was driven by a mom named Penny Giakoumis, who was three months pregnant and on her way to daycare to pick up her toddler daughter. The Subaru's front bumper caught Lyle at the knees, causing his skull an instant later to fracture as it punched its way through the windshield, heading for the item seat-belted by Penny into her front passenger seat. This item was a large espresso coffee machine. The machine had a protruding lever attachment. This polished steel lever entered Lyle's head, penetrating to a rough depth of four inches as the rest of Lyle's body continued its journey into the passenger seat, the upright back of which was slammed into a reclining position, leaving Lyle and the coffee machine as much in back seat as front and the steel lever still embedded in his brain.

The police estimated that Penny's car had been travelling at roughly 60 km per hour, or 10 km over the limit — not an uncommon infraction. There were no skid marks. She ran the red light. She couldn't explain why. She mentioned the rain and the fact that she had glanced at the rental contract lying on the seat beside the coffee maker. She didn't see Lyle until he was entering the vehicle. She suffered bruises and a fractured kneecap when the Subaru continued across the sidewalk and smashed into the wall of a bank building. (The airbags deployed with this impact, saving Penny from more serious injury.) Lyle lived for five days in a coma, and then his heart failed. They said he had probably been unconscious from the moment his skull broke through the windshield. No one else was hurt.

Penny Giakoumis managed to contact me months later by email, with a message of abject remorse that almost made me sympathize. Her life had been altered too. She had to that point still avoided jail time. My thought — my feeling — was that maybe weekend incarceration for, say, five years, would be appropriate. She was, after all, a mother with responsibilities. But she had also driven at full speed through a red signal at a busy intersection. She could have destroyed a dozen lives if the odds had been stacked right. At least I felt no share of guilt. The minor flashes of it were quickly dealt with by my rational mind. There was nothing I could have done to prevent the accident, short of telling Lyle, for no reason, that he should not leave the house that day.

I later heard through the lawyers that Penny had given birth to a healthy baby boy. The news caused me to go completely bonkers for ten minutes. My vision went white. My brain froze. I nearly stopped breathing. When I could form a thought again, I began charging around the empty house, shouting, "Lovely! Fuck! Well, the child is just fine. Fucking fuck fuck fuck! Isn't that lovely for dear Penny? She must be happy. Happy! Penny is happy! With her healthy baby!" and so on, while I dragged books off the shelves and knocked over two wing chairs and picked up a lamp and swung it like a baseball bat at the newel post in the front hall. That made me stop.

10

Mirza gets the email report from Kemo and then a day later from his father: Halid's bones have been released to Kemo's family. They plan to bury them in the Muslim cemetery above Kovači, fifteen minutes' walk from Mirza's family apartment. Adem's other news is that he is still sharing the apartment with two older cousins, sisters. The cousins are supposed to move out, but it has been delayed. They've been resident since just after the war, but now their house in Žepa is finally being rebuilt, and they're moving back. Mirza knows only that Žepa is somewhere in the Bosnian outback. He's never met the cousins. He's not thrilled at the thought of him and his dad sharing a two-bedroom apartment with them and hopes they're gone before he arrives.

Kemo later sends Mirza a picture taken in the cemetery: himself and a friend at Halid's grave, standing grim-faced on either side of the marble pillar carved with his name: JAŠAREVIĆ HALID 1975–1994. Behind them hundreds of the square, salt-white gravestones march up the hill. The photo reminds Mirza that Kemo's father also died in the war. At the edge of the frame is an identical pillar bearing Ismet's name. Kemo has something new in the photo: a full beard, identical to his friend's. The cut of them signals devotion.

During Kemo's summer stay in Toronto two years ago, he and Mirza visited a Bosnian mosque in the western suburbs. The building was a disused warehouse and looked it, without even a proper minaret. After prayers were done people gathered for a meal, and it became clear that some of the men were married to Serbs. A few children even had Serbian names. Later Kemo said the place was little more than a Bosnian social club. When Mirza suggested this was better than bringing the divisions of Bosnia to Toronto, Kemo's response was basically, Sure, why not? Let's just forget the war ever happened.

Mirza bristled: "You think I'm forgetting just because I'm Canadian?" They were sitting on the deck, Kristina at the back of the yard with the hose, trying to revive her tomato plants. "You think we move here and then Bosnia just disappears?"

Kemo looked at him. "You moved, we stayed. Our lives are different. I'm not saying it was wrong to move away."

They left the subject for lighter talk. It seemed their sporadic postwar emails, for ten years plus, had kept their friendship stuck in adolescence. The face-to-face reconnection in Toronto began to change that.

❖

Mirza sits with the map of Bosnia spread across his mother's kitchen table: a crisp new Austrian folding map with a level of detail the Web can't begin to match. Incredibly, this one shows even tiny mountain villages and the peasant footpaths joining them. His mother is cooking, cubing beef for a weekend stew. She's pretending indifference to the map, to his interest.

He's finding the names of towns and places he remembers visiting or hearing about in childhood. Now he can actually see where they are, how near or far from Sarajevo.

"Mostar. Did we ever go there?"

"We went through sometimes, on the way to Makarska."

"We never stopped?"

"Once or twice maybe. You were just a baby."

Mirza stares at the snaking highways intersecting the town, the little grid image of Mostar streets. He knows they recently rebuilt the destroyed Turkish bridge. It caused a global media blip about Mostar and the war. Prince Charles came and made a speech about the meaning of bridges.

His mother is quiet. Mirza shifts his gaze to the coast, up the Adriatic highway.

"I wonder if Dad's been to Makarska yet."

"Would we have heard?" She lets the comment hang, underscored by the clacks of the knife blade. "I hope you see Makarska again, and Baba and the family. All for the good. The rest, I don't know."

"The rest?"

His mother gives him a flat look. "The other part, the Sarajevo part. I don't quite see the point. You'll work construction for a month or two and then come home."

"Why are you pretending? You know it's not about that."

"Yes. Your art. Your installation," She paces out the word. "You don't know what goes through my mind. You don't seem to care."

"I do. Of course I do. It's in my mind too."

"Mirza that is hardly possible. You were a child."

"I don't have an imagination?"

"But why — why would you even try to imagine these things?"

"What things? What are we talking about?"

His mother dumps the meat into the pan of hot oil and abruptly swears, shoves it off the flame, streams tap water over her hand.

"You all right?"

She shuts off the tap, examines her hand. "After all this time ..." She shakes her head. "For what? Is this about your father?"

Something turns over inside Mirza, a thump.

"Could be. Partly. It's everything. They found Halid, for one thing."

"Halid."

"Kemo's brother."

"I know who he is."

"They found his remains."

"All right. Well, I'm sorry."

"It doesn't bother me. I mean it does, but it's part of the whole thing. It's like the teeniest part of the whole massive fuck-up."

"You're acting as if I'm ignorant."

Then his mother does a mother thing. He feels it coming a mile away. She comes and sits opposite him at the table. Her eyes are filled with some misguided idea of his pain — the knowingness in them. He drops his eyes to the map, the tangle of roads and borders and rivers.

His mother says, "You could talk about this. I don't mean with me. To a group. Maybe — maybe we should have sent you a long time ago. We thought; wait and see."

"I'm not a child, and this is not about therapy."

"But being with your father won't help. I can't imagine. Back in that apartment? It will only get more complicated."

"How is that possible? I mean, look at us. Look at this family."

His mother's gaze flares, then seems to blank out.

Mirza says quietly, "I remember *Deda*. That day. I remember when you came back from your friend. From Grbavica."

A pulse of breath escapes his mother. They never say this word. That place. After a moment she gets up. She goes to the stove and slides the pan of meat back over the flame. The small cooking sounds seem to fill the room.

He says, "Something happened, because you were a Serb. Yes?"

"Don't talk about this."

"I'm only —"

Kristina turns and leaves the kitchen. Not even angrily. She slips out like a ghost. In a moment he hears the click of her bedroom door shutting. If she slammed the door, it would be easier, it would make more sense.

Mirza feels the hot tingle come at the corners of his eyes. He presses his thumbs there and makes it stop. He moves to the stove and shuts off the gas, covers the pan and sets it aside. He goes and stares at the open map, and it pulls him away into the shadings of soft green and yellow, the red highways he will drive. He folds up the map and stores it safely away. Before he leaves the house he puts a note on the table: *Sorry.*

His mother is a Serb. They never speak about it outside family. Mirza remembers his grandfather saying it the day of the killings at the church: that he and Kristina were Serbs and that it mattered. Once it mattered and was spoken, there was nothing that could make it un-matter. The war came, and overnight, victim or not, it was shaming and exhausting just to be an ordinary Sarajevo Serb — suspected by your neighbours and shot at by the gunners up in the hills. Kristina never called herself Serb in Bosnia and knows never to mention it in Canada either, where people will simply lump her in with the ethnic cleansers. All these years later, people still get that twitch in their eye when they hear the word.

He should not have let his mother see his studio photos. Pictures miss the point, obscure it. Her interest in his work has always been peripheral anyway. Same with his father. Adem is not interested in remembering the war, not with his son. He has his army buddies in Sarajevo for that. Mirza's mother was in a group once, women who talked about their war issues, but she has never talked about these things at home. At one point Mirza and Teo went together to check out a Muslim group in their high school. They were the only Bosnians at the meeting, both of them only half Muslim. Given that they were Sarajevans, they were not even real Muslims to this group. They were white Euro boys among Arabs and Pakistanis and Sri Lankans.

And now Mirza is going to Bosnia, with his firmly Muslim name, and he will be there with

Adem (the playboy romping free in their old city, their old apartment), the two of them back in the ancestral land in a town filled with Muslim survivors and a few Serbs with suspicion always hanging over them. There is little about any of this that they can share with Kristina, except the charade that Adem is making money and will someday bring it home.

Walking down toward Greektown he phones Jen and leaves a message. Miraculously, she calls within seconds — to say she'll have to call back. She tells him again to use texting. Maybe he will have to give in, not so much for Jen but because Teo and others are on his case about it too. So he'll have to join the dweebs who are never in public without their thumbs twitching away, head slumped and earbuds in, as if it's the physical world around them that's the fantasy. Now Jen is on Twitter. She's on it when they walk down the street or sit across from each other in a restaurant.

She calls back, and they agree to meet at seven for a drink, maybe dinner. Jen makes like she is slotting it into her busy evening. It's obvious that their plan to try again was never real, not for Jen and, Mirza can now see, not for himself either. He's only avoiding the unknown. But that has to stop.

He has about a half hour to kill. By now he's

approaching YuRock, so he just swings in without much thinking about it. His father used to drink at this bar, except when someone turned up who seriously annoyed him, like some Belgrader or dumb Canadian who thought he understood Bosnia. The place is pretty quiet on weekdays, and Adem liked to flirt with the owner's twentysomething bartending daughter. Adem steers clear of male Serbs who aren't proven friends, but an attractive *Srpkinja* is not something he'll reject out of hand.

Tonight, the place is empty except for a man at a table with probably his kids, two girls, one only a child and the other just beyond child, with hips and breasts. They are eating McDonald's takeout. The dad is drinking beer and stealing fries. He nods at Mirza just because they are the only customers. Mirza thinks he'll have one beer then head down to Danforth. But the bartender is nowhere to be seen. He stands at the bar and glances up at a basketball game on the flat screen.

She comes in from the street door, lugging a six-pack of tonic and a jug of orange juice.

"Be right with you."

"No problem."

Ana, that's her name. She stows the mixers in the fridge and takes his order.

"Mirza, right?"

"Right."

"Ana."

"*Znam. Šta ima?*"

"Ah, you know. Place is too quiet. It needs to pick up. Your dad still in — where is he?"

"Sarajevo."

"Girlfriend."

"Yeah. Business too."

"Can't be too easy."

"He's doing all right. He has some questionable friends."

Ana takes a moment to catch it. She laughs, "*Pa, on je hajduk.*" An "outlaw" she calls him, a word used by kids playing cops and robbers.

An old man comes in and joins the dad and daughters. His baggy pants and cardigan look like he could have worn them driving a cab in Sarajevo. He passes out some lottery scratch cards to the girls, and they lick the burger grease from their fingers and set to work with their thumbnails. Ana excuses herself and goes to their table.

The few times Mirza has been here, Adem's presence helped make up for the stained wallpaper and the stale air, the feeling of limbo. The place could sometimes get a pretty decent crowd on weekends. His father would argue back at guys whose opinions he though were bullshit. He was calm but firm, sure of his facts. Mirza watched cocky, uninformed dudes buckle under his power of words. Adem also knew when, at a certain point of tension, it was time to casually leave or maybe just buy a drink for the ignorant or the legitimately bitter.

Ana talks about the neighbourhood. "It's Arabs and Afghans now. Halal butchers. There's a new mosque out by Greenwood. The Yugs are moving to the burbs, Mississauga."

To Mirza this is not worth lamenting. There are thousands, tens of thousands, of Toronto Yugoslavs, but there was never a Little Yugoslavia, not really — just an invisible fringe of Greektown with a few delis and bakeries and struggling bars. There was a Bosnian bar over in Cabbagetown for a few years. Mirza went there with his father the summer he turned legal and the ritual beer initiation with the kid was happening — as if the kid had never got drunk before. The war was closer then.

There was a night when one man, older than Adem, a Sarajevo Serb, was talking about being forced to dig trenches and load bodies into trucks, how he'd been a professor and a pacifist and this is was what he was reduced to. Later he dropped his pants and showed Mirza the amazing scars all up and down his leg, like the muscle tissue had been carved away and the skin re-glued over what was left. The guys around him hardly reacted — it was like: there he goes again. This was at the point when Mirza was feeling his most Canadian and the leastever connected to his homeland. A room full of dadlike men drinking beer and swearing in Bosnian made him feel twelve years old again. The drunken ex-professor with his weird chicken leg just seemed sad.

Something changed. He had parcelled it away as just an adult thing, a parent and soldier thing, all this brooding and raking through the rubble. Then, in his mind, it shifted from old and sad to freshly tragic. Teo's dad too was a professor who refused to carry a gun, and he was shot dead in a Mostar street by a sniper in the first months of the war. And Kemo: his dad blown up in a trench, his brother captured and tortured. Mirza can see that Teo is like Kristina, that his choice is to bury it all and be Canadian. For Kemo, still in Sarajevo, forgetting is hardly an option. It's a good thing, not to forget. They do it at Auschwitz for the Jews. Why not for the thousands and thousands murdered in Sarajevo and Višegrad and Mostar and Srebrenica?

He finishes his beer. Ana is sitting beside him on the customer side of the bar, texting and playing video poker. The table of McDonald's diners have left. Mirza puts some cash on the bar and stands up to leave.

"Come back, eh?"

"I will. Eh?" He underscores the "eh" and gets a half-grin.

At Pappas Grill he finds a table on the patio and orders beer. He waits till 7:15, then 7:30, 7:45. A bit later he leaves and starts walking. He moves through scents of grilled meat and garlic and knots of strollers, holding a westward course all the way to Broadview and on across the Viaduct. When Jen calls, he stares at her number a moment and then kills the connection. A warm wind is whipping through the anti-suicide cables lining the bridge, making a deep hum he hears at breaks in the traffic. Jen phones again. He takes the call and doesn't even say hello.

"Fuck off, okay? It's over. That was the last time. Don't call back and don't leave messages. I won't listen."

It's good. Instant relief. He can feel the sweet smile creeping onto his face. What a liberation. So simple. To begin ignoring each and every phone call from her. Striding on across the bridge, he is walking away from her, from it. The air rushing past his face is full of tree scents from the valley. It seems the same temperature as his skin. As he walks he decides where he's headed. He presses forward, the lush summer smells filling his nostrils.

He has been to the bar before, shared a beer there with his uncle Alex when they met to talk out his issues with his parents. There are no issues to discuss now. It's time to move out. It will be good for him and his mother both. He'll be leaving for Bosnia in less than a month. He can stay at his uncle's when he comes back, until he makes some decisions about the long term.

Mirza hits Kemo's number. It's about two a.m. in Sarajevo, and he gets the answer service.

"Hey, it's Mirza. I just ditched my girlfriend. Remember Jen? You can forget her now; it's all over. Um, another thing: can you maybe stop sending emails about horrible Serbs? Alija is guilty too, right? Don't forget. See you." He wonders if that was a bit much, the crack about Izetbegović. But it irks Mirza, Kemo lumping his mother together with bloodthirsty Serb nationalists.

Mounting the steps to Woody's, he wishes for his uncle not to be there. He pulls open the heavy door and walks through to the rear bar and takes a seat partly obscured by a pillar. The bartender is loading beers into a glass-fronted cooler. He is younger than Mirza, looks barely out of high school. He chucks the bottles into place with professional verve.

All of his encounters with Kemo, maybe six or eight at the most, occurred in the empty apartment across the landing. This was in the last months of the war, a limbo time. They were thirteen, Kemo closer to fourteen. The abandoned flat was a ruin: a huge hole blown out of the wall, furniture gone or smashed apart for firewood. There was an old foam mattress. They would just drop their shorts and play. It didn't take much action to bring on a climax. The whole thing could be over in three minutes.

He'd had his first-ever orgasm on that mattress. Slick white fluid on his stomach, the bleachy smell, Kemo grinning weirdly. They shot jism at the wall like it was a contest. It stopped because freezing weather came and made it not worth the pleasure gained. They never talked about it. They were kids with exciting new toys to play with. Boys did this stuff. Some boys got harassed if they were too obviously fixated — or sissies. But the sex itself was just a dirty joke. It didn't mean you were some kind of alien.

Canada made it different, made his brief thing with Kemo a whole way of being, of having an identity to be defended. Gay was discussed in health classes. It was about rights and stigma. Mirza sidestepped all that when Carli Bryer seduced him. Carli had been matched with him as a "peer tutor" to help with his English, but at their so-called tutorials in her mother's condo they didn't use language much at all. Sex was sex, and it turned out to be fun with a girl too. With Carli it became more imaginative, more adult.

He went from Carli to Tatiana, who was Russian and exotic and funny, then eventually to Jen in his last year at OCAD. There was the one-off with the guy at the artists' colony in Banff: Ray. Ray the video artist, summer of 2005. After two weeks, on the last day they went hiking. Mirza knew Ray's reason for proposing the hike, and he let it happen. They jerked each other off in a stand of evergreens halfway up a mountain with a panorama of rocky peaks staring at them. It was his first encounter with a dick that wasn't his own or Kemo's, a dick with a disturbing sideways curve. Then back home to Jen and the unspoken, increasing awareness that they were wrong for each other. They lurched along, making no plans and irritating each other, right up until she kept him waiting an hour at Pappas Grill.

The bottle-blond bartender, Tim, has a dimpled smile and insanely white teeth. Mirza orders another pint. The crowd is growing, shifting from after-work unwinders to the pumped-up night crowd. Even just a week ago he was still thinking these desires needed no expression. The denial seems kind of pointless now, with Jen gone. It's the reaction of others that's the issue. He will have to come out, or play the bi card or — what's the word? *Polyamory.* Meaning, essentially, it's all cool. He feels that he maybe won't do anything tonight. He's watching the flirting and gabbing men and still feeling above them, outside them.

    He stays until closing time, then hovers outside. He's waiting for the bartender. He waits a long time and almost gives up, telling himself that bartenders are paid to flirt, but when at last he comes out, Mirza blurts a "Hi." Tim stops, looking him up and down, performing it.

Mirza says, "Where you headed?"

They walk the short block to Tim's. Mirza is only moderately drunk, or thinks he is, but it seems enough to open him to new things. Without discussion, Tim appears to understand that Mirza is entering new territory. For Mirza it's not quite new. It feels something like arriving home.

He wakes in Tim's ridiculously sun-drenched studio apartment high above Jarvis Street. He quietly gets out of bed and showers. As he's searching for his clothes in the cluttered room, Tim's eyes open and observe him, and he feels a twinge in his exposed cock, but Tim rolls over and after a moment sits up and says, "I'll make some coffee. Don't go away."

Mirza dresses and sits on the couch, watching his host wash two enormous oranges and slice them into wedges. He can catch the peel scent from across the room.

"Come to the table," says Tim without turning around. "Cream? Sugar?"

"Just black."

They eat. Mirza asks Tim's family name.

"Why?"

"Just curious."

"Kurstic."

"Tim Kurstic. Would that be more like Krstić?"

"Yeah, Krstić. Tiho."

"That explains your coffee pot."

Tim's gaze flicks to the copper *džezva* atop his fridge. "I never use that."

"So are you from Bosnia?"

"Croatia. Knin. You?"

"Sarajevo."

"I was in Sarajevo once. I was maybe five years old. You remember the war?"

"I was there for the whole siege."

"So are you a hundred per cent Muslim or ...?"

"My mother was Serb. Is. You?"

"I'm Canadian. I was nine when we left. I don't ever want to go back there. You still hungry? I might make some pancakes."

"Seems like a lot of work."

"Pancakes? They're a snap." He gets up and briskly clears away the plates of orange peel, then gets organized for pancake making.

Mirza says, "I've never done, you know, penetration before."

"Oh? Well, it wasn't obvious. Much. You seemed to enjoy it."

"I was pretty drunk."

"Uhh-huh ..."

The way he says it, Mirza has to laugh. He watches Tim work.

"I'm going to Bosnia next month."

"Why?"

"My dad does construction there. I haven't been back since I was a kid. My best friend from school still lives in Sarajevo."

"You know what they think of queers there, right?"

"Yes. But I'm not ..."

"You're not ..."

"I'm not planning to advertise it. And I'm not — not necessarily, one hundred per cent ..."

"Whatever."

"Whatever. Right."

PART TWO

11

In the first week of 1945 on a snowy hillside in Montenegro, Pero's father caught a German bullet. He died a hero for Tito's Partisans. Months earlier his mother, grazed by a bomb fragment on a Sarajevo street, had succumbed to septicaemia. At only fourteen Pero was orphaned. Too young to fight, when peace came, he signed on with the Tito Youth: clearing rubble, rebuilding roads and rail lines, delivering food to camps filled with refugees. He shared the family apartment with his older sister until she married and moved away, then his widowed aunt and three young children arrived and stayed for months. There was weeping and shouting. Pero spent more and more time with his Brigade comrades, avoiding his own home and bed that now felt not only invaded but also a daily reminder of how irreparably things had changed.

Two years with the Brigades helped earn him a small scholarship to the university. The militarized rough-and-tumble gave way to lecture rooms, hours alone in the library, and discussions in cafés beginning with coffee and ending long after dark with beer and brandy. History was Pero's field. The matters discussed were pressing: how could Marxist thought be best applied toward the future of Yugoslavia? The culmination of centuries was at hand, the true plan just beginning. What exactly *was* a Yugoslav? They had much to learn and much to contribute.

Pero happened to be sitting with his student pals one warm night in a Sarajevo *ćevap* house when a group of foreigners came in, most of them female, and took over a nearby table. They spoke English, but one of the young women switched to the waiter's tongue each time he came round. Pero knew she was not a born Bosnian before even a full sentence was out of her mouth. Her way with his language had the inflections of what might have been Dalmatia or Zagreb. She wore a summer dress covered in small blue flowers, no stockings, and also, it appeared, no makeup of any kind. Her unblemished face and clear eyes seemed to him almost fresh as a child's but animated by the ironies of someone who'd lived. Pero nursed his beer and let his sidelong gaze consider the crevice under her crossed thighs, where the flimsy dress had ridden up. Her warm skin rested on the wood of the chair. When he glanced at her face, he saw that he'd been caught. It seemed to amuse her. Then his friends took notice and the catcalls began.

On nights when he could manage it, Pero went

alone to the café with a few rehearsed English phrases, until he found her there again, this time with two women. He moved to a vacant table near them. As he ordered his beer, she acknowledged him with a glance and an aside to her girlfriends, and then it seemed everything (though he couldn't catch a word) was about him: how amusing he was, or inadequate, or too young, or perhaps just too Bosnian. He drained the last of his beer and with a clumsy effort got out of his chair and found a coin, but he dropped it and had to get down on his knees to search — a complete disaster. His face was on fire. As he left he cast her a final glance and was sure he saw regret in her face. He went back a week later, to the hour, and found her alone at a rear table.

Mara was from England, a translator on a one-year posting to Bosnia with the Red Cross. Years before, the Croatian Fascists had forced her Serb family out of Zagreb and they'd landed in Southampton.

Mara put Pero's fumbling encounters with schoolgirls into perspective. One of the first English words he learned from her was *virgin* — he was, she wasn't. Pero more or less ceased studying and saw her daily, for weeks. Because she was billeted with Red Cross workers in a school dorm, they met always in his family apartment, the main tangible thing left of his pre-war life aside from his married sister in Banja Luka. He had never lived anywhere but in this apartment on Despićeva Street. With his sister and aunt gone, the three small rooms and kitchen were his alone. Mara brought some life to them again.

After years of war and hardship, his glimpses of rapture with Mara seemed almost an impossibility. As the pitch of their pleasure waned, other impulses began to alter and deepen. Nightly acrobatics seemed unneeded. They had sleep to catch up on and duties to stop neglecting — Pero his studies, Mara her work with Bosnia's struggling populace. She still had most of a year left in her Sarajevo posting. When their love proved tenacious, they began to talk about her summer return to England. They decided Pero should come with Mara to Southampton and be introduced to her parents. Through an old army friend of his father's now with the Foreign Ministry, Pero managed to get student travel papers.

In July, Pero entrusted the apartment keys to a neighbour and embarked on a series of first-ever experiences that instantly revised his relations with Mara. Though they were only four years apart, he became more like a gaping child to her indulgent, worldly mother. Pero had never before crossed a border, never spent days and nights on a train, never heard German or Italian that wasn't barked by soldiers. He had never boarded a ship, nor vomited over its rail into the English Channel. He'd never eaten battered fish atop a golden mountain of fried potatoes oozing grease into yesterday's newspaper, which he did, ravenously, on a bench by the Southampton quay as Mara held their place in the interminable customs queue.

He became the live-in guest of Petar and Gordana, Mara's parents. Petar's field was metallurgy. As war approached and they were forced from Zagreb, he'd parlayed his expertise into a research posting at Southampton University. Mara said it had probably saved their lives. Petar's formulas for carbon steel eventually went into British munitions.

The house faced a swath of meadow and trees: the Common. Pero began learning his Anglicisms: *hob*, *Wellingtons*, *chap, mac*, *Marmite soldiers*. Being Serbs, the family didn't eat Marmite soldiers, but they enjoyed describing Marmite's qualities to Pero and watching his look of nausea. He was assigned a bed in a gabled room on the top floor. He did his morning wash-ups hastily in the busy bathroom on the middle floor, making himself a visible but unobtrusive part of the family's jump on the day.

Without much discussion of the matter, it seemed to be decided that Pero would make a worthy son-in-law. Petar used some university connections to get him work helping to cart thousands of books out of wartime storage and back into the rebuilt library. Pero was made an assistant on the rebinding team. The work, the bookish company, the books themselves, all helped his English to develop rapidly.

When first-born Aleksandar came into the world, Pero and Mara had been married three years and still lived in the family home. Pero meanwhile was on his way to a degree in Slavonic studies at University College London. He spent weeks at a time away from Mara and the baby, living in a cramped bedsit. On occasional weekends, he took the train to Southampton, a small part of him regretting the quiet hours stolen from book work. At home the baby's squalling kept him awake. Mara questioned him, as if idly, about his London days and nights, but the truth was he had nothing to hide beyond an occasional pub night. Returning on the train, his bag was heavy with Gordana's preserves.

The Cold War spurred a wave of scholarly interest in Eastern Europe. With Petar's influence, Pero got a teaching post in Southampton's fledgling Slavonic studies department. They moved into a row house not far from the Common. The neighbourhood was a mix of surviving and postwar homes and a scattering of weedy lots that still held rubble from the Blitz. It surprised Pero that Southampton had endured almost as much destruction as Sarajevo. Hitler's reach had been vast.

Pero and Mara were eventually able to arrange an annual lease on a house in Dalmatia. The seaside town of Makarska became their summer home. Long after Kristina and Aleksandar had left for new homes in Bosnia and Canada, they still holidayed there each year.

There had been a girlfriend Mara drank coffee with in the mornings. The woman, whom Pero knew only noddingly, became a godsend during the last months of Mara's lymphoma, driving her to appointments and sitting bed-side with her during Pero's working hours.

After the funeral, Krista and Alex stayed on for several days with Pero until he finally encouraged them to return to their lives. What he needed, in fact, was privacy. Of course, with the best of intentions, friends and neighbours sometimes breached that. Mara's coffee friend came by one day bearing a large shepherd's pie still warm from the oven. He made a pot of tea while she brushed away tears and said she did not know what to do now in the mornings, or who to have lunch with in the high street. It was as if she wanted to draw out Pero's grief, but he kept a firm grip on it. When she had recovered somewhat, he sought advice about house cleaners.

Pero did not much cultivate friends and had none he could honestly call close. He returned to work within a month. Back in his university office he could see that, essentially, work was his closest friend. It calmed and focussed him immediately. Most students were either ignorant of his loss or simply uninterested. The distressing issue was the behaviour of colleagues. They approached him with probing eyes, then their gaze would waver, as if he might fracture under observation. As he fell without much effort into his habitual scholarly engagement, his ironic asides, the others became their old selves, the tacit agreement to ignore his bereavement almost instant.

At night he went home to a house that smelled faintly of fried breakfast instead of imminent dinner, where he would turn on the lights and sit through the evenings trying to read, staring at the walls or the television when he failed. He in fact spent hours staring at the walls, the furniture, the carpets, the pictures, recalling how the objects had come to be there. They were the remnants of what seemed a long dream. The things in the house were unchanged, but the meaning of them was now more a mocking preamble to the prying force that began to visit him. He sat late into the night and examined the force in between its manifestations. It arrived and it filled the space around and inside him. Its essence gathered in his gut like a poison, then it would push up and burst from his throat in waves of sound that could not be stopped. He thought of the neighbours: hearing and pitying him. He thought of the wailing women from his boyhood in wartime. It was as if they had returned to possess him and drive him mad. But the force would always leave. It would stay half an hour, maybe an hour, then move on, like a storm receding across empty fields.

Among Pero's colleagues and his loose social circle were a few unattached women. Eight months after Mara's death, with the autumn term underway at Southampton, he felt the brisk air and the tang of turning leaves giving him a familiar lift. He got a haircut, spruced up his wardrobe, and launched some completely unprecedented efforts at flirtation. Women whom he'd shared shoptalk with for years met his overtures with blank stares. They retreated into scrupulous collegiality. When Pero fell back to his usual distance, he and everyone breathed a sigh of relief.

He became resigned to his new life: making his bed or not, living on eggs and sausage and tinned soup, augmented by frozen dinners after one of the pitying colleagues gave him an old microwave oven from her cellar. From the beginning, the oven gave off a faint smell of dead rodent during use. He learned how to heat the frozen meals in his gas oven instead. Occasionally, Mara's coffee friend brought him a casserole. She would arrive with an air of jaunty busyness and, he was glad, would not cross the threshold. Once, he cooked himself a roast of pork with boiled potatoes and peas and gravy from a tin. He had a frozen cream pie to finish. The meat was dried out, and the whole exercise, from shopping to washing up, felt absurd. He never repeated it.

Pero felt less and less a part of his own world. His students increasingly bored or irritated him. His scholarly work fell to a picking over of the ideas he'd risen on years before. At home, he cracked open and abandoned novels and history books. Television only seemed to underscore his aloneness. Kristina began sending him videos of Yugoslav films from Sarajevo. Watching some of them, in particular the war stories, brought on an intense nostalgia. The melodramas of wartime comradeship and Partisan heroics suffused him with memory and longing.

At sixty-one, Pero took early retirement. He sold or gave away everything but a few photos and mementos and left England, returning to the city of his youth. The wars of Yugoslav secession had run their brief course — the laughable one in Slovenia and the fierce one in Croatia. Sarajevans firmly believed that war could not visit them. The city was a model of harmony. The Winter Olympics had put them back on the world map. Bosnia itself had always been Tito's showplace, living proof of the power of Yugoslav Brotherhood and Unity. A referendum on Bosnian independence was coming up, its results all but certain: Bosnia would secede and be internationally recognized.

In the calm of this collective denial, Pero arrived at Adem and Kristina's walk-up flat with a taxi full of luggage. He was delighted to get firmly reacquainted with his only grandchild, nine-year-old Mirza, whom he'd hardly seen since his toddler years. He began to take daily walks in the city, confirming its solid presence and reasserting his own. On Despićeva Street, the old apartment block still had its scattering of pocked craters in the stones of the facade, a souvenir of Hitler's war.

Eight years before, the year of the Olympics, Pero had stood in the same street with Mara, looking up at the third-floor windows. Behind those panes his childhood had unfolded. Later, in those same rooms, he and Mara had fallen in love. They stared up at other people's lace curtains and empty flower boxes, the flakes of a light snowfall drifting into their eyes. Then they'd walked a few blocks through the icy streets to the agreed-upon café to meet Alex and Lyle for lunch. The meal had been marred somewhat by a table of loud Germans and Lyle's overly fussy demands on the waiter. Pero couldn't understand his son's attraction to this man, but over the course of the holiday, Mara had helped him adjust to the fact of it: Alex and Lyle were a couple, with all the apparent comforts and difficulties. The main departure was that they both knew how to cook. Together, on the last weekend of their stay, they'd whipped up an impressive meal in Kristina's kitchen, though the roast had been underdone for Pero's taste.

Now, each time Pero passed by Despićeva 4 on his morning walks, he still felt its odd pull: strangers up there moving around in the familiar rooms, with different curtains, new cupboards, more layers of paint, but certainly the same careless loves and regrets, all of it as reliable as stones and mortar. If he could climb again to the roof, he would see the twin towers of the Catholic cathedral just a few streets away, and the spire of the Orthodox church, and minarets in almost every direction. He didn't believe in any of those gods. Like his father's, Pero's faith was in Sarajevo's cultivated indifference to clans and religion. On the tram cars of the old circle line, he could still rub shoulders with Ivans and Dušans and Muhameds. He saw his city still intact, defying the old memories of wartime and the new, fanatic nationalists.

With the tram service extended now even to suburbs near the airport, occasionally Pero's outings would range far enough to take him out past the aging apartment blocks of Grbavica, to treeless expanses with coldly lit supermarkets and rows of new high-rises staring at one another's blank faces. It amazed him that a dwelling offering a view of tonnes of concrete and cars piled up at signal lights was anything that a person could call home. Pero's Sarajevo was in the streets and cafés of the city centre.

Not long after his arrival at Kristina's, he was back in touch with a few of his old childhood chums and his comrades from the Youth Brigades. It seemed a miracle that this vanished world still lived and breathed. Under the creased faces and grey stubble were Šaban, Mika, Vlatko, Koča. He took pleasure in hearing and pronouncing the names in such rare supply in England. He was invited to dinners and football matches and country weekends. He sat with his friends at café tables, and they drank coffee and repeated anecdotes. They discussed the news and the politicians braying about old crimes and nationhood. They had varied opinions on whether war was imminent. Then it was upon them.

Pero was sitting one day in Kristina's kitchen eating a lunch of sardines and rice. He had just told Mirza to run and get his newspaper from the sitting room. He heard the shell coming in. There was a roar, and he was hit hard in the head, and he saw a blinding flash of white. That was all.

12

Mirza's life changed overnight when his grandad was injured. Pero came back from the hospital and was bedridden for weeks, needing constant care. Mirza was required to contribute. There were fits of temper, both his own and his mother's, but they adjusted. He emptied his grandpa's urine bottles and bedpan — literally a pan, from the kitchen. His mother sponge-bathed Pero in bed while he helped her shift legs and arms. Mirza had to wash Pero's cock and balls and bum while his mother stood at a distance giving instructions.

It soon became clear that Pero was able to move on his own but needed encouragement and direction, or, what finally got him going, ultimatums. Kristina devised mandatory exercises for him in the bed, which triggered his own variations. Then he was sitting up, then standing and shuffling to the toilet, batting away helping hands. From the day he came home he was talking about the distant past like it was happening right there in the room while they fed or washed him. Gradually, he became able to dress himself, sit and eat a meal, and more or less get himself through a day unaided. But they still had to listen to him or, if they could, tune him out.

Adem was mostly away at the front, so he was rarely a part of these things. He hardly ever entered Pero's room, which had been Mirza's room until his grandad arrived from England. Mirza got used to sleeping on the daybed in the main room. All of these routines were turned chaotic during sustained bombardments. Sometimes they spent days and nights in the cellar of a newer apartment block down the street, crammed in with dozens of mothers and kids and old people and the smell of urine and sweat and shit.

Whenever his father came home for a few days, the centre of attention shifted completely to him: the fighter who needed to be recharged. Sometimes he did nothing but sleep day and night with breaks for food. Kristina cooked best when Adem was home. They didn't always know when he would show up, but as soon as he was through the door, she started cooking, making the best from what was on hand. A hot sit-down meal, even just rice and beans, seemed to make Adem look around and remember who he was, to remind him he was a husband and father.

Of course they argued. They howled at each other. One time Kristina hadn't got water, and she was cooking, so she asked him to go out, and he shrugged and took the plastic jugs and much later came back in one of his smiling-dangerous moods where everything was just fine, no problem, but he moved around like a set trap until some small thing tripped it and he was shouting about what he sacrificed, what he faced each day, and how she couldn't leave her precious father for only the time it took to get water for her own husband and son, and so on.

Sometimes, if he got very drunk, he threatened to wallop her, said she needed to "wake up." She dared him to do it, but he never hit her that Mirza knew of. His voice always gave away that it was a hollow threat — and his pose, with a clenched hand raised behind his head, stretched so far back it showed how little he wanted the fist to connect. Even Pero, who watched the fireworks and threw in ignored comments, seemed to know that Adem would not really hurt his daughter. Pero's face just looked sad and knowing, like he knew every turning point in the battle and that, regardless, he could not possibly have an influence.

Mirza feared disaster from their fights. Every time, he thought his parents might really harm each other, destroy what little they all had, just from the violence of the words themselves. His mother would go from screaming like a madwoman at Adem to weeping extravagantly in a corner, then Adem would storm out, or if booze was available, he might drink alone in the kitchen staring at the walls until he was passed out with his head on the table. They slept separately for a night or a few nights until Adem went back to his unit.

It was obvious to Mirza even then that his parents were in totally separate worlds, and also that Adem's world out in the war was closed to him and his mother completely. Sometimes he arrived drunk and happy-sad, full of kisses, sometimes just grim and resentful, looking at everything like it was an insult to his pride. Within minutes, he would be raging about something, the food or some little task not being done, spoiling their happiness at the mere fact that he still lived. Or he locked himself in the toilet for hours with the portable radio, the volume cranked way up, until Kristina had to bang on the door, pleading.

Mirza's father never talked about what happened to him in the trenches, except only once that Mirza remembered. This was when his school friend Bajro was killed. He came home with a wristwatch and a gold ring, and he went out the next day to take them to Bajro's family. When he came back much later he broke down at the kitchen table. He lowered his head and clasped his hands behind his neck. He made no sound at all, but Mirza could see his tears on the plastic tablecloth. Kristina stood with her hands lightly resting on his shoulders. To Mirza she looked almost serene, even though she was crying too. She bent over to kiss the crown of his head. And, of course, Adem must have cried when word came of his brother's death, but Mirza strangely has no memory of that. He remembers his father going away at some point after the war ended, to visit the place where it happened.

If there wasn't much action in the trenches, his father came home lugging firewood from the hills. Mostly, they had to scrounge in the city. One day, Adem showed up while Kristina was out searching for wood. She came in with a few sticks, scraps of furniture. He was washing in the cold kitchen and he grunted a hello and kissed her, and when he looked at her little pile of kindling, he put his coat back on without a word and left with the axe. They were wearing winter coats indoors because their only regular source of heat was small tins of cooking fuel from the aid packages. Adem came back after a while with a split door, just like the doors in their own apartment that they'd already burned. He dragged the pieces in from the hall and chopped them up for the stove.

Early the next morning a man came and demanded his door back. His teenage son had sold the door to Adem. The man and Adem had an argument on the landing that escalated into a fist fight. Kristina and the other man's wife were shouting for the men to stop, but they didn't stop until they were bleeding and exhausted. This was another time when Mirza saw his mother serene and crying, afterward when she was washing the blood off Adem's face and he was still swearing quietly, drinking shots of the same brandy that was on the rag cleaning his wounds. His father the warrior, defender of country and family. He poured a mini-shot for Mirza and watched approvingly as Mirza drank it like water, scrunched up his face, and coughed.

Kristina finished up her nurse routine and sat watching Adem pouring nips from the bottle, taking it measured now as he brooded. She watched his face and said she had to go away for a few days to help someone. Adem watched her with the same pensive look, rolling the brandy on his tongue. Mirza asked for another shot, but they completely ignored him.

This was when something happened to his mother. There was some sort of ceasefire and Adem was on a longer leave. His mother went to see her friend in Grbavica who had a health condition. Adem wasn't happy, because he was left to cook and take care of Pero. Kristina came back haggard and hardly spoke. There was a visit to the hospital. There was a night when she became hysterical and it seemed to go on for hours. She collapsed on the floor wailing, and Adem got down with her and wrapped himself around her, and she fought him. It passed, like everything else. Adem told Mirza that some men had detained her, locked her up for a while. But that's all he would say.

13

Kristina calls me a few weeks before Mirza's departure date. She's been reading her son's email and has found links to what she calls "war porn."

"Horrible stuff. I can't tell you. It's coming from his school friend who was here, Kemo. He seems to be some kind of extremist, and now he's trying to draw Mirza into it. I think that's one reason he's going back. Working for Adem is an excuse."

"Are you leaping to a conclusion, Krista?"

"You should see this stuff. I'll send you the links."

"I won't look at it."

"Have you seen his project?"

"I think his work is obviously against violence, against extremism."

"I don't see how it can help people who went through that."

"It's for people who didn't."

"They can get it on the Internet."

"But that's not art."

"You think what he's doing is art?"

"Why not? I'll admit it's disturbing."

"We came here to get him away from that. His friend has become a full-time Muslim by the sound of it. I'd call him a fanatic."

"If Mirza knows you're reading his mail —"

"I've stopped."

"He's an adult, Krista."

"I know, I know." Krista's voice falters.

"I talked to him about going. He's committed to it."

"Talk to him again."

"He's already got his ticket."

"I'm sending you the links."

"Don't do that."

"Just look at them."

Kristina sends video links, which I ignore. I do look at her cut-and-pasted quotes from Kemo's messages, which to my mind don't sound particularly extremist. Kemo wants justice.

The murderers are still with us. They are unpunished, still walking among the ones who they could not erase from their failed Serbian utopia. They took away my childhood. They killed my father and my brother. They destroyed the youth of my friends.

❖

I come onto the front porch with Pero's orange juice, and he looks me in the eye: "I want to go home now."

"You are home. This is your home."

"Don't lie to me."

"Why would I lie? We live here, all the family. It's home."

"Sarajevo is home."

"We're here now. I never lived in Sarajevo." I state the facts as good-naturedly as I can. I return often to these recitations, give up, come back to them again. "*Tata*, listen to me, please. You lived with Mama in England, in Southampton, for forty years. You raised me and Krista, your son and daughter."

"Krista."

"Yes, Kristina. Why do I call you *Tata* if you are not my father?" He squints at me. "I'm Aleksandar. I'm Sasha, your son. This is our house."

"You cannot be my son."

"Why not?"

Pero laughs incredulously. "You are too old!"

I stare out at the garden sodden from a morning cloudburst, peonies bent double and pasted to the flagstones. Several houses down I see the mailman approaching. All of this has happened before. Again,

I will show Pero the printed evidence, impressively delivered by a uniformed government man. The mailman arrives in his rain-slicked poncho with the Canada Post logo. He gives me a handful of damp mail: junk and two letters, both addressed to me. I hand these two to my father.

"I am your son, Aleksandar Banjac. You are Pero Banjac. You see the address? It's here on the house. Look here, *Tata*. Number fifty-seven. This is my home, our home."

I leave Pero staring at the letters and go inside. In less than an hour I'm expected at the library. I put on some coffee for the home-care worker I am expecting any minute. When I come back out onto the porch, the letters are on the chair and Pero is gone. I go out to the sidewalk and scan the length of the street. I walk a block in each direction, checking front porches and looking between the houses. I come back and check my side gate — locked, as always. Pero is not in the backyard. As I go back inside for my car keys, I call the library.

I cover the immediate neighbourhood, driving at a crawl, peering into yards and alleyways. The sun is out now, raising steam from the wet pavement. Pero will certainly have his wallet in his pants pocket, with his ID and a card with my own and Kristina's cell numbers. I remind myself that he is safety conscious. He obeys signals and stays on sidewalks. He would have no cash, no way to buy streetcar tickets or pay a cab fare. He would be wandering on foot, as he did on the two occasions he took off from Kristina's house.

The first time, a neighbour recognized Pero and jollied him into her kitchen for coffee while she got a message relayed to Kristina. Pero's second break took him almost into Scarborough: a St-Hubert's BBQ franchise. The miles of wandering must have made him hungry. A call came, and while the restaurant kept him plied with food, I drove out to pick him up. Pero had reportedly asked them how to get to Sarajevo. It must be about two years since the St-Hubert escape. Pero was beginning to seem trustable.

Honking from the car behind urges me through an intersection. I methodically retrace my search route, then expand the circle. Soon I turn onto Kristina's street. Could Pero have found his way here by some homing instinct? He lived at the address for more than ten years. But Krista would be at work now, and Mirza probably at his studio, and Pero has no key to enter the house. I park and do a search of Kristina's front and rear yards and the garden shed. I knock at the rear door and then the front, then let myself in. The house is empty. The crisis still seems to be my secret.

I recall something about a bar, a Yugoslav bar on Pape Avenue. Adem and Mirza have gone there. I can vaguely picture it though I've never been inside. Have they ever taken Pero there, maybe to share a beer with other war vets? Pero's war stories might even be interesting to someone who hasn't heard them a hundred times.

I cruise down Pape scanning the storefronts, then loop back and do a slower pass until honking starts again. I swing into an empty spot by a fruit market. Outside on the sidewalk, a youngish man is stacking oranges. His profile, hairline, even his by-law-defying cigarette all say to me, "Yugoslav." I lower the passenger window and call out, "*Izvinite!*" The man glances at me.

"*Ima li Jugo bar ovdje?*"

"*Ovdje?*"

"*Blizu*. I mean nearby. Here on Pape. It's called Yugo something."

"Yeah, yeah, it's there." He points down the street. "YuRock."

I can just make out the sign.

"Ah. Thanks."

"Not a problem."

The man watches curiously as I get out of the car. It was odd, of course, spouting Serbian out of the blue on a Toronto street to a complete stranger. I can't recall having done it before.

YuRock's frontage presents a broad pane of dark-tinted glass. Two scuffed plastic chairs sit near the entrance. I'm about to try the door when it opens. A young woman props it wide, smiles vaguely at me, then disappears into the dark interior. Bar smell wafts out. I step inside to see the woman propping open another door at the rear. A flat-screen TV shows a muted soccer game in progress.

She moves behind the bar and flashes another working smile: "Give me a minute."

"It's all right. I'm not drinking."

"Coffee?"

"Actually, I just need to know: was there an elderly fellow here in the last hour or so?"

She drops out of sight and comes up with a tray of demitasses.

"We were locked up."

"I don't know if you know Adem Osmanović. He may have been here with my father."

"Could have. Adem?"

"A tall fellow, kind of wiry, fortysomething. From Sarajevo. He's back there now in fact."

"I know who you mean. His son was in."

"Mirza."

"That's the one."

"I'm his uncle. I just thought my father might have come here on his own. He — he wanders."

"I get you. Sorry. Haven't seen him."

"If you do happen to see him, I mean a confused-looking, elderly fellow who talks about Sarajevo or the war, I mean, you know, the *old* war, Nazis, Partisans ..."

"Sure."

We exchange phone numbers, and I go out to

find a $30 ticket on my car. I drive back to Kristina's and let myself in. When I go into the kitchen, there is my father at the table, spooning pink ice cream from a bowl. He glances at me indifferently. I can see Mirza out on the back deck pecking at his laptop. I head out.

"Hey, Uncle Alex. What's *Deda* doing here?"

"Did you phone your mother?"

"Huh?"

"Please just tell me if you talked to her about *Deda*." I try to squelch the tension in my voice.

"No. What about *Deda*?"

"All right. I just — I dropped him here while I ran some errands. I meant to give her some advance warning."

"Trudy saw him on the porch. He must've locked himself out."

"Trudy?"

"Neighbour. She has a key."

"I see. Well, thank goodness she noticed."

I sit across from Mirza. He is focussed again on his laptop screen. He swears and clicks it shut.

"My mother's been reading my emails."

"Are you sure?"

"Absolutely. She didn't even cover her tracks. She read stuff from Kemo even before I got to it."

"Kemo from Sarajevo."

"Yes."

"Nothing too compromising, I hope."

"Just the jihad connection."

"Jihad? Is that a joke?"

"Of course. What do you think?"

He exhales loudly and looks across the yard. I can see a tally of indignities working their way through his features.

I take a casual tone: "She's concerned of course, about your going over there. In fact, she asked me to talk to you."

"That is bull, Uncle Alex."

"What, that she's worried?"

"That she should be snooping into my life and running to you about it, like Kemo is some kind of extremist wacko. That's her own baggage that's talking."

"Maybe, yes."

"Kemo is a friend since before school. Way back. His war situation was bad. If he says something about what Serbs did, he has the right."

"I guess I agree."

"You guess?"

"I do agree. I'm sorry, Mirza, I just want to save some grief for your mother, if I can."

"Okay, well, I'm sorry too. But I can't change whatever fantasy she has in her head."

I start to speak, but Mirza rides over me, his voice quavering.

"It's like she assumes I don't have the same rights as her. To work stuff out. We got completely fucked over. All of us. Her included. Things happened. There were reasons for it. She might want to forget it, but I don't. The fact that Bosnian people were just expendable peasants in some backwater."

"Mirza, I don't think —"

"But that's what happened."

"That is in part what happened, yes."

"She can't deal with it."

"Everyone has their own way."

"Exactly."

Then he is out of his chair and down the steps to the yard. He walks in a circle, staring at the grass.

My father has come out from the kitchen. He pulls up a chair and sits across from me, still with the ice cream spoon in his hand. He says, "I am a professor of history."

I experience a light inside my head, a small flash of white.

"Yes, *Tata*. You are a professor. Where did you teach?"

"Oxford."

"No. But close. You taught at Southampton."

He stares at me. This is a memory from his blank period, the middle years. This is not supposed to happen out of the blue, with no triggers. Mirza is watching us from the yard.

"He remembers teaching, Mirza."

"What?"

"A memory, from Southampton."

"Oxford. He said Oxford."

"England. He remembers."

"It's from the *book*, Uncle."

Pero stands and goes into the house. I follow him to the kitchen. On the table is his *History of Bosnia*, the Oxford Press paperback. Kristina's copy. The memory was only a few moments old. He is now at the sink rinsing his spoon.

"You were reading, *Tata*."

Pero stares at me with a blank face. He returns his attention to the sink. I go back outside.

"You're right. He found the book."

Mirza comes up the steps: "That shell should never have hit *Deda*. And then we were supposed to be grateful they drove him to the hospital."

"They?"

"The UN. The Protection Force. It's like, the cops sit around in their cars all day watching people get beaten to death, and then they help clean up the mess."

"It's not quite like that."

"It was like that for the whole damn siege." Mirza stares hard into something. He looks at me. "My mother would be fine now, *Deda* would be fine, if they'd just bombed the Serbs when the war started. Just stopped it. No siege of Sarajevo. No Srebrenica."

14

The gravestones are luminous, crystalline in their pure whiteness, blinding in the midday sun: a forest of shimmering, chest-high pillars climbing the grassy hillside above Kovači's warren of stucco houses. Mirza's climb with Kemo through the twisting streets from the mosque has left his forehead slick with sweat. Today's was his first-ever visit to the small neighbourhood mosque, though it stood just a few steps up the street all through his childhood.

Kemo's mother is now moving up the slope, ethereal in pale blue. She seems to float between the stones, silk lifting in the hot breeze. She stops, her head angled at a marker, and extends her hands with palms up.

"She comes every day. Early, before heat. Today she waited for us."

"Do you come too, in the mornings?"

"No. She needs her private — her privately."

"Privacy."

"Yes."

Across the road is a smaller plot of graves,

older, the stones dingier but more ornate, many with turbaned tops. Mirza knows these from his childhood. The larger graveyard is completely new to him.

"So, Miki, why we are speaking English?"

"You started it."

"You would like to speak Bosnian?"

"We could. Maybe one or two big words I won't get."

Kemo smiles the smile of his ten-year-old self, with the same scary-looking incisors. "You never use big words in Canada?"

"I've been speaking English for twelve years. Except stupid arguments with my parents — those are in Bosnian."

Kemo laughs, still with the donkey-like intake of breath that made him a target in school.

Majka is floating down among the white pillars. They walk back through the narrow lanes. Majka veers off to do some shopping, and Mirza is conscious that he's about to be alone with Kemo in their apartment — the first time in twelve years he has set foot in the Jašarevićs' family flat. Kemo is talking about the friends he wants to introduce later. There's a plan to meet in Baščaršija for an early dinner, just after late-afternoon prayers. Kemo prays five times a day, a practice Mirza simply can't wrap his head around.

Kemo and his mother still live in the same

third-floor flat across the small courtyard. In the war, the families shared a clothesline that spanned the ten-metre gap, and when the boys were stuck for days or weeks at a time indoors, they sometimes used it to reel notes and even snacks back and forth to each other. The sagging plastic line is still there, and the metal pulleys at each end where Adem mounted them on the iron railings.

Mirza and Kemo climb the concrete stairs. By the window on the first landing is the spray of shrapnel scars on the sill and the cement floor, painted over but unmistakable. A neighbour lost her legs. They pass over the spot, and Mirza sees Kemo catch his eyes glancing down and away. The past twenty-four hours have been studded with these moments, each triggering a weird time warp in Mirza. He wonders now if the maimed neighbour still lives behind the door one flight up. As they pass by it, he sees the claw marks low on the door. He can't recall the family's name, but the dog's comes to him right away: Garo, a goofy black mutt. Like many dogs, he was finally left to fend for himself in the street.

Kemo opens the apartment door and motions Mirza into the narrow vestibule. There is the antique coat stand with the mirror and the hole for umbrellas. There is the painting of the arching Turkish bridge. Mirza can see now that it's a print, probably bought on a weekend jaunt to Mostar, maybe even hung in that spot before Kemo or Mirza were born.

"Place hasn't changed."

"Not too much. New carpet, only past month, from Istanbul. My mother goes to see her girl-friends."

"Turkish connection."

"It is one great city. We can be same. Smaller, *naravno*."

"Naturally."

"But Turks are not so serious about Islam. Coffee, yes?"

"Yes."

Kemo goes into the kitchen. Mirza stands, taking in the mix of new and familiar. The dining table looks the same, even the chairs, which have to be replacements — he recalls sitting on plastic crates after the family burned the originals. He goes into the toilet and quietly shuts the door. The familiar patina of grime around the brass latch plate. This was the one door too necessary to burn. He stands peeing. The windowsill: thick white gloss of paint, the hardened drips on the under-sill. He reaches to pull the cord, and the water flushes and gurgles. The same, exactly. From the kitchen he hears the whir of an electric coffee grinder. That is different. But he did notice the old hand grinder still in its place above the stove.

Why didn't this rush of sensation happen when he stepped into his family flat the day before?

There he merely felt blank, numbed by the familiar everywhere and his father's insistent, vaguely manic talk about the building projects he had lined up, where he'd be posting Mirza. He would have to get a temporary driver's licence. Did he bring his Ontario licence? All right, it would do for now. Already Adem has scheduled him to begin driving truck on the coming Monday to some town hours out of the city. At least his dad's cousins from Žepa have moved out. Mirza is sleeping in his old room again, though he had to strip and remake the bed himself, once his father managed to find some clean sheets.

Kemo has the coffee pot and cups and sugar on a tray and is moving toward his bedroom. Mirza follows. Though Kemo and Halid were almost five years apart, this was the room they always shared, and it still looks like a boys' room. Kemo puts the tray on his desk. Against the other wall, Halid's desk holds only a small row of books, a jar of pencils, and a framed photograph of their father. Kemo sits on the lower bunk. Mirza chooses the chair at his friend's desk. He looks out the open window. A woman opposite is washing down her balcony railings with a bucket and sponge.

"You still not take sugar?"

He looks at his friend. "Still not."

"Coffee came from Istanbul — with the carpet."

"*Najbolje.*"

"Best, for sure."

This room was their private sanctuary once Kemo's brother went away to the front. The rare times Halid came home on leave, the space was ceded to him, to his moods and day-long sleeps, his solitude.

Kemo gets up and pours the coffee.

"It's strange. To be here again."

"Of course."

"I feel outside of it, you know? Except ..."

Kemo sits on the bed and blows gently over his steaming cup. "Except?"

"It's like I'm in a dream, visiting what I was."

"Not was. What you are."

They sip at the strong coffee, the same coffee Mirza's mother still drinks in Toronto, boiled in a copper pot, thick with finely pulverized grounds. Mirza usually prefers his own filter drip. His gaze goes to a patch of sunlight on the carpet. Among the patterns is what looks like a toy car or truck. Then he sees others, each like a little joke in its nest of whorls and tendrils.

"You have trucks on your carpet."

"Tanks. They are tanks for battle. Afghanistan. My uncle, he bought carpet there. Some years ago."

"Soviet invasion."

"No. After."

"Right, Soviet thing was eighties or something."

"Correct."

Mirza feels odd speaking in English with his

old friend, but his Bosnian seems childish compared to Kemo's. His schooling in Bosnian came to a virtual halt at age nine. His father was not a reader, and his mother's books were mainly English. When he ventures phrases to Kemo now in Bosnian, Kemo smoothly redirects them back to English. Kemo is proud of his English ability. Meanwhile, Mirza's father has been firing Bosnian at him since the moment he landed. Back on the home turf now, Adem has of course completely abandoned the Toronto "English at home" rule. It was really Mirza's mother who insisted on it.

"Now the Afghan tanks are against Americans."

Mirza considers this. "The Taliban have tanks?"

"Secret weapon. All on carpets."

"A good place for them."

"Agree."

Mirza tries to picture the uncle, the one who was absent so much.

"Which uncle do you mean?"

"Uncle Jusuf. You must remember."

He does remember. Jusuf was the wheeler-dealer uncle who went to live and work in Saudi Arabia — who spent the whole siege there with his family. He was there when his brother, Kemo's father, was killed in the last weeks of the war. From Riyadh, Uncle Jusuf had tried to impose a by-the-book Islamic funeral for Ismet, on a family that, like Mirza's, had been loyal Titoists, indifferent to religion. It was all about which side, which set of believers, should own the funeral rights. Everything was changed by the war. It made atheists obsolete, turned them into dusty relics just like Tito himself. Somewhere along the line, Kemo and his mother became believers. In fact, didn't Kemo spend some time in Riyadh after the war?

"You visited him."

"In Saudi? Yes, I was living there. One year. Mother came also."

"And your sister."

"Short time only. She did not enjoy." Kemo shrugs.

Mirza looks into his coffee cup, then out the window at the black-scarved woman still cleaning her balcony. He says almost to himself, "I don't believe." When he turns his head, Kemo is smiling knowingly at him.

"It doesn't hurt. Allah makes no pressure. The man must choose." He sits back on the mattress. "I will give you some books."

Mirza levels a finger at him: "Pressure."

Kemo laughs. And then they are talking about dinner plans.

Mirza lingers in the shade of a tree in the mosque's spacious forecourt. Kemo and his three friends have washed their hands and faces at the spigots and are now bowing and praying under the columned portico. In a smaller section of the broad porch, a few women sit on the steps or do their own devotions. He has forgotten the proper name of the gazebo-like washing structure, but the mosque's name is ineradicable: *Gazi Husrev-begova*. It is centuries old, imposing, the stones time-worn: one of the city's Ottoman treasures.

Mirza has never prayed. Not in any mosque or church. He has never even attended a religious service in Bosnia that he can remember, unless he counts the one burial he was allowed to attend during the siege: for Kemo's father. He has only the vaguest clue about how to pray, but he is watching Kemo and friends with interest. Facing the back wall of the portico, they bob their heads and bend from the waist. A few minutes later they remove their shoes, place them on the shelves provided, and enter the mosque through its high central doorway. Two of the Kemo's friends are actually wearing jeans. None, despite Arab-style beards, are in the sort of robes you might see in Egypt or Iraq.

Dinner is at Željo's. They sit round an outdoor table, and like a tourist Mirza orders beer with his *ćevapi*. As the word comes out of him, he realizes that Željo's has never offered alcohol.

"Maybe you are still in Toronto?" one of Kemo's buddies says amiably.

"*Ne. Ne više. Ja sam Bosanac.*"

His Bosnian reply brings a tumble of words from the group, studded with jargon he can't catch. Mirza simply grins and nods. The group is clearly a close one, ribbing and playing off each other, stopping to probe Mirza in English. One of the friends, Damir, doesn't speak much, but when he does, he reveals English at least as good as Kemo's. His eyes seem slyly appraising.

The food comes and they settle to it. With Bosnian in his ears and late sun slanting on the cobblestones and tile roofs, the scent of greasy charred meat and fresh-chopped onion, the whole scene comes to Mirza as a sensory time warp. He looks up and sees Damir staring at him with a twitch of a smile.

"I remember now. Yes." Damir puts some bread in his mouth and chews thoughtfully. "You are Miki. I know. I know what your father did. Really brave guy." Damir flashes a grin and a thumbs-up and focusses again on his food.

"What did my father do?"

Damir just keeps quietly smiling and eating. The others seem vaguely curious but the moment passes.

Kemo says, "Damir was neighbour."

Mirza nods. He's starting to form a memory of Damir. One of the others speaks up.

"Kemo told us you were in the siege."

"Whole time, yeah. In Kovači. You?"

"I was in Serbia. Prijepolje."

"Lucky guy."

"True. But now Sarajevo is better place for us."

Damir says, "I am from Višegrad." He stares at Mirza, working the food in his mouth. "Višegrad Serbs burned my father and brother when I was seven. But I got away, with my mother and sister. How is your life in Canada?"

"Too boring. That's why I came here."

Kemo takes up his tone: "He's going to build the pyramids."

"With my father, yes. It's true! Tourist centre in Visoko. My dad thinks there's money. Maybe inside the pyramid? I don't know."

It's good to shift from war talk, see the faces relaxed and smiling again.

After the meal the group splits up. Mirza still has a hankering for beer and asks Kemo where they might go. They walk through the low wooden shops of the Turkish market and out into Ferhadija, with its Austro-Hungarian facades and sleek glass storefronts. To Mirza the broad promenade is still Vase Miskina, even though it's since been renamed to honour a destroyed mosque. There is barely a bullet hole or shrapnel mark still visible on this street, with the exception of two or three starburst scars preserved in the asphalt outside the Catholic church. One still has traces of the commemorative red resin applied just after the war. They called them Sarajevo Roses. Mirza's father used to mock them, say they were for gawking tourists, as if they had any right to them.

Behind the church, they cross over the tram tracks and continue on. Kemo leads the way. At one point he breaks a silence with the word *Markale*, tilting his head at a small square filled with food stalls. Mirza looks and tries to recognize the place. He knows he was more than once at Markale market with his mother. People later died there as they shopped, targeted by mortar bombs.

They follow along the tramway until Kemo turns them into a narrow street. He leads Mirza through tall wooden doors into a long boxcar of a room with a vaulted brick ceiling. From the look of the crowd, they could almost be in a Toronto bistro, except for the haze of cigarette smoke. The room is crammed with antiques and curios, softly lit by dim bulbs in dusty chandeliers. They find a free table close to the bar. Kemo calls out an order: Sarajevsko beer for Mirza and coffee for himself.

"When are you to start with your father?"

"Monday."

"Pyramid Centre?"

"Some other place, near Doboj."

"No pyramids in Doboj. Or in Visoko."

"I know they're probably fake. But so is the shrine at Medjugorje. People still come."

"Your parents, how they doing these days?"
"Complicated."
"They are split?"
"Yes and no."
"How yes?"
"Canada ... Bosnia ..."
"That is wide split."
"We don't discuss the Bosnia thing. My mother hates my coming here. She wants to forget everything."
"Forgetting, remembering, it is all one thing. Like DNA. Double helix."
"Hey, you're a smart guy."
"Absolutely."
"What she really hates is the project, the installation. People react to it, to the idea, so I don't talk about it much. It has to be seen."
"I saw. You sent pictures. You forget?"
"Those were early. I'll send you some when I go back, maybe a video."
"Toronto atrocity show."
"It's more. Not only about atrocity."
"I hope."

The beer and coffee come. Mirza touches his glass to Kemo's cup and says "*živjeli!*" — "cheers!"

"Soon you will speak only Bosnian."
"Only if you stop speaking English."
"For one day, English; for next, Bosnian. I like to practice. Now say me, how it is more than

atrocity only."

Mirza sighs. He can hear what sounds like Italian from a nearby table. The chattering crowd is eclectic — arty twenty-somethings right up to grey-haired professor types. At the bar are two guys in hipster jeans and modish jackets. No one, Italians and mods included, would be out of place in a College Street café back home.

Mirza says, "It's about more than bloodshed. It's about process. War as money, as media spin, as politics."

Kemo shrugs, "Mladić, Karadzić, Milosević."

"And UN. NATO. CNN. Of course, criminal guys like Ćelo and Caco too."

"Agree." Kemo nods. "But biggest problem is Serbs. Ninety per cent."

They watch each other's faces.

"You mean ninety per cent responsible. Not ninety per cent of all Serbs."

"Yes."

There is a hesitation in Kemo's "yes." They break the gaze. Mirza stares into his beer glass. Kemo says, "Maybe eighty per cent responsible, but not less."

Mirza won't pursue this numbers game. He knows that for Kemo, Alija Izetbegović is still a Muslim hero, *the* heroic leader of the war. He looks around for distraction and catches one of the hipsters scoping him. The glance quickly veers away.

"You know where to bring a guy."

Kemo smiles curiously at the comment. They sit, watching the crowd. The music is an odd mix: Motown, Sinatra, Dylan, Billie Holiday, just loud enough to energize the room. Maybe he has brought Mirza here to show him how cool Sarajevo is, how un-Balkan, but Kemo seems just slightly impatient, or out of his element, like he's waiting out the duty of bringing his guest here — cheerfully enough but still wanting to get back to his real life. There will be evening prayers in a few hours, back at the mosque.

"Miki, you remember Damir?"

"Yeah, sort of."

"They moved into your building, in nineteen ninety-five. Little guy."

"Right." Mirza nods with the dawning memory. Damir was the kid who moved into the wrecked flat across the landing, with his war-widowed mother and sister. They had nothing. Neighbours scrounged some furniture for them. It was probably just a few months before Mirza's family left for to Canada.

"Damir is here only for summer. September he goes back to Tuzla for the university. He maybe can help you about Srebrenica, for your art."

"He was in Srebrenica?"

"Whole wartime almost. Until the massacre."

"He did the march, over the hills?"

"Serbs let him stay behind with mother and sister. He was only a boy. But some family were killed, older cousins."

"Many?"

"Come again to Željo's after mosque. Maybe he will talk more."

They sit, mostly in silence, watching the lively crowd. Mirza finishes his beer. He senses from Kemo that this signals departure time.

"You would like a second Sarajevsko?"

"*Ne. Samo jedno.*"

"Okay, friend, I have to go now. Sadly. There is a meeting." He gets up and goes to the bar to pay. Mirza stands to go, but when Kemo comes back, he sits and begins rummaging through his shoulder bag. He brings out a book with a green cover and bold white lettering: *Young Muslims of Bosnia*.

"For you. In English."

Mirza flips through the first pages.

Kemo says, "History for hundred years."

"Great. Thanks."

"Welcome."

Mirza stows the book in his backpack, and they go out into the dusky evening scented with car fumes. At the corner by the tramway, Kemo stops.

"So, I am going other way. You know way back?"

"Of course."

They shake hands. Kemo keeps the contact brisk. He goes right and Mirza left, back toward his father's apartment.

15

"I saw the Jahorina house only once. When we were there for the Olympics. Snow up to the windows. You were just a babe — I mean in the British, not the American sense."

Mirza enjoys hearing his uncle's quirky Anglicisms after two weeks with his father.

Alex continues, "Though I don't doubt you've encountered a few Bosnian babes."

In fact, Mirza has had no time for cruising Sarajevo babes. If anything, he's been wondering more about the potential of some of Kemo's friends.

"I'm on the road mostly. These are the first days I've had off. It was Kemo's idea to check out the ski house."

"How is it? Still in the family?"

"There's no house, just walls. My bedroom has a tree growing in it."

"Must have been a shock."

"I knew it was destroyed. I just wanted to see the place again. It belongs to Serbs now, the whole area. Ratko Mladić used to bunk in the ski lodge."

"I see. Best not to tell your mother that."

"I haven't talked to her."

"She's here, in fact. Want to say hello?"

"Sure. Of course."

Mirza hears his mother being summoned. He prepares himself to be upbeat, to coast through.

"Hello, Mirza." Her voice is tender, tentative.

"Hey. How are you?"

"Oh, busy. Thinking about you, of course. Alex is making us some dinner."

"How's *Deda*?"

"He's doing fine. You're all right?"

"Yeah."

"And your father?"

"We're good. I'm his wage slave, basically."

"Aha. Well ..."

"It's strange to be here, definitely, but — I don't know what to say. It's a trip."

"Yes, well, it would be."

"The city looks good. People are out in the cafés all day. It's, you know, *vibrant*."

"I'm glad."

"I'm reconnecting. Neighbours are still around, some of them."

"Did I hear the word *Jahorina?*"

"Yeah, we drove up this morning."

"How did it work out?"

"Great. It's in RS now, but that wasn't a problem."

"And the house? Is it ...?"

"Gone. Pretty much. I took some pictures."

"Oh? Why? You took pictures of the ruins?"

"Yeah, the ruins. I won't send them to you or anything."

"That would be appreciated. Were you with your father?"

"Nope."

"Alone?"

"I went with Kemo. It was his idea actually, to go."

"I can imagine his take on it."

"Really. What would that be? Like a radical take?"

This leaves a moment of dead air.

"Please let's not argue, Mirza."

"I thought it was worth seeing, worth facing."

"Fine. That's fine." Her tone is limp.

Mirza sighs. "Christ," he says under his breath.

"Never mind. I don't mean to —"

"It would be nice just to have a normal conversation."

"We may differ on what that means. What normal is."

"What do you want me to say? How pretty the mountains are?"

"I guess I'd like that, yes."

There's a tight pause, then they both start talking, pushing the words through, negating each other.

His mother inserts a phrase that has irked him since childhood: *more than you bargained for.*

"Is your father there?"

"He's been in Zenica for a week."

"I suppose it's bound to happen."

"What is?"

"You'll learn things."

"Uh-huh. And?"

"Do you have a cell number for your father?"

"Of course."

"He's not answering email."

"I can't give out his number."

"Then just tell him please that we need to talk."

"Right. A conference about the kid. I'm twenty-five years old."

"It's not about you. It's him and me. Mirza? Are you there?"

Mirza can accept that they need to talk. Or that his mother does. He tells her he'll pass on the message.

"Thank you. There's another reason. Tell him Aunt Hana called me from Makarska. They've decided to move your dad's mother to an apartment. She's okay, just can't deal with the stairs anymore. They've been trying to reach Adem."

"I'll tell him."

"They want to discuss selling the house."

"Baba's house? They can't do that."

"I'm sure Adem won't let them."

"I love that house."

"Yes. I think we all do. Alex and I have been talking. He has an idea to take *Deda* to Makarska next year. The doctors say it might help him recover the blank period. A place of strong memories, positive ones, not like Sarajevo. It was always our favourite place, years before I met your father there. We could make a family holiday of it."

"That'd be good."

"A kind of reunion."

"I'll talk to him. He's not answering much, but I'll keep trying."

Mirza is viewing the photos he took at Jahorina. There is not much to inspire nostalgia, but now the yellow electric service box, still bolted to the wall of the gutted house, triggers a memory: a childhood snapshot, himself and Kemo squinting in the sun beside the box, and attached to it an old Red Star football decal Mirza had found in a drawer. His mother must have taken the picture. Later his father arrived, a little drunk maybe, and saw the star and said they would not support any team from Belgrade. This morphed into a monologue about Communism, and how the time for red stars was gone. Mostly he seemed embarrassed that the neighbours would see it.

Mirza zooms now on the image. He thinks he

can actually see the damaged paint where Adem scraped the decal off. He's sure the snapshot still exists in a family album. Most of those photos went with them later to Toronto. Maybe some didn't.

Mirza goes to the sideboard and opens the bottom drawer. Among the old tablecloths and saved gift wrap are two albums. He takes them to the dining table. They are the oldest ones: white-bordered pictures curling up from brittle black pages, family faces going back even to his grandparents' childhood, faces he recalls only as the images themselves and maybe the sounds of a few names spoken over them when he was a little boy. These are Osmanović albums, from his father's side. One includes some wartime snapshots taken at a forest camp: Partisan officers with red stars on their caps and lapels. There are uniformed women too. Shots of destroyed houses. A horse pulling a wagon full of debris.

Just before he flips to the back cover, Mirza can visualize the image glued to it: a yellowed picture of Marshal Tito clipped from a newspaper. He is sitting on a shelf of craggy rock somewhere in a battle zone, one arm in a makeshift sling. They had to memorize the details in school: Tito was wounded in 1943 on Mt. Ozren. He refused transport to the hospital camp and carried on leading his fighters against the Fascist invaders.

16

Mirza's father has construction links to at least six sites, some of them hours out of the city. For weeks he has been away from Sarajevo more often than he's been there, issuing text messages from Visoko or Zenica or places unknown while Mirza loads and delivers building supplies. Then, out of the blue, he shows up at the apartment, has a shower or a meal, maybe a night's sleep, and heads out again, leaving Mirza a meagre handful of cash for his labours, the bills an unpredictable mix of tattered Bosnian marks and fresh euros.

One afternoon, Adem comes in unannounced from Zenica. Mirza is masturbating on the sofa, hears the key in the lock, and barely has time to put a cushion over his lap. As his father breezes past and into the kitchen, he's smirking. He tucks into some leftovers from the fridge and tells Mirza to get dressed for work, as they are heading out to deliver a load of paving bricks to the Pyramid site in Visoko. In the truck Mirza tells his father the family news from Makarska.

"Sell it? No way. The house stays. Why didn't someone tell me?"

"Did you check your inbox?"

"Fuck."

Adem pulls the truck to the shoulder. He punches in a call and waits.

"Are you calling Baba?"

"I don't want Baba. I want Ivo."

Adem leaves a pointed message for his brother-in-law: he'll be driving to Makarska tomorrow for a meeting about the house. If they've contacted property agents, they are to cancel immediately. He pulls back onto the highway.

"What did your aunt say about Baba? Is she okay?"

"She can't deal with the stairs anymore."

"Is she still in the house?"

"Don't know, Dad."

"I'm away a few days and everything changes."

"Can I go with you tomorrow?"

"There's work to do here."

"Would be nice to see Baba."

"Later."

"Dad, I've been over here, what, a month? I haven't seen her. Not since I was thirteen. When would I have been there?"

Adem turns, and his eyes hold on Mirza's, then shift back to the road: "We'll go. We will see her."

They arrive with the interlock stones, and there is no one on site and no equipment to shift the pallets. Mirza and his father pile the bricks into wheelbarrows and wrestle them up a dirt path to the rear of the site. The building is still only a foundation surrounded by dry mud. They work in silence. The day is muggy, and sweat pours off their faces. Kids on bikes stop to gawk at them.

Talk of Bosnian pyramids tends to make the local people roll their eyes. Two or three of the hills near Visoko have a striking pyramidal shape, but the excited claims and the global media have come and gone. Mirza's father is with the camp that is still gambling that tourists will ignore the debunkers. He and his partners have visited the real pyramids at Giza, Egypt. They even found a Syrian archaeologist willing to hype the project for a promised cut.

As they haul and stack the stones, Adem breaks the silence with bursts of swearing, then he gets on the phone and lets Mirza keep working while he paces and argues and barks demands at message boxes. Mirza feels like he might faint from heat stroke. They finally get it done and sit in the shade, gulping from a litre bottle of warm fruit juice.

"Fucking Zijo said he's working. Cunt. He's sitting in his *kafana* in Mostar."

"What happened to the loader?"

"Fucking stolen, for all I know."

In Bosnia his father swears just like the old

days, like all his war vet buddies. Mirza doesn't have the facility or even the inclination. It's just one more thing to make him feel twelve years old again, his father drunk and in from the trenches.

They climb back into the truck. Mirza drives. His father smokes and makes phone calls until his battery dies, then he delivers a monologue to the windscreen. How the house in Makarska is a cash machine they should have been renting for years to the beach crowd. How he'd told them it was unsafe for his mother, being there by herself with a heart condition, but no one would listen. The rental income could have paid for a retiree apartment for Grandma with a healthy profit on top.

"We'll get Ivo sorted out. Hana can't stand up to him."

"What if Baba wants to stay?"

"Stay? What, live on one floor and use a bucket? Wash in the kitchen? No. It's time to go. Better now." Adem sighs and stares ahead at the road. In the familiar way he begins tenderly touching his head above the ear where the bullet, years ago, scooped a groove in his skull.

It's almost dusk when they come into the city. They park the truck in the supply yard and get into Adem's red Škoda. They are famished, but with nothing much in the apartment they just shower and change and walk down to Baščaršija. At a hole-in-the-wall place with tables out on the cobbles, they share a large cheese *burek*. Then they order *ćevapi* and finish them off. When they're done, they sit staring mindlessly at the evening strollers.

Adem says, "Any plans? Meeting up with your Wahhabi buddy?"

"Why do you call him that?"

"You mean he isn't?"

"He's just Muslim. *Salafi* is the word. Kemo is the real thing, you know?"

"Words. Come have a beer with your old man."

"What, it's time for a talking-to?"

"I was joking, Mirza. I think you can handle Kemo."

Adem picks a café in the busiest stretch of Ferhadija. The Friday night crowd flows past in an unbroken stream: young guys in small groups, couples young and old, elderly men or women in ambling pairs. Mirza has no desire to binge, but his father seems intent on steady drinking. He feels his face acquiesce into the dutiful half-smile he wears for nights like this, when his dad insists on pursuing oblivion. As Adem puts away two beers for each one of his own, Mirza lets the passing throng take his thoughts. The Bosnian faces make the rare foreign profiles stand out. Bosnians, the younger ones, male or female, seem to him definitely among the best-looking people on earth. Adem is talking about construction setbacks and how they don't really matter.

"Did you hear me?"

Mirza looks at his father. "Yeah."

"We can work through the winter. Just get a roof on it and do the inside jobs."

"Don't we need walls first?"

Adem stares flatly. "Don't smart-ass me."

Adem's eyes are taking on a glassy look, his head tilted back, scoping the crowd. He rambles on about floor joists, doorframes, corrupt inspectors, reaches for his beer, lights up cigarettes, all without any break in the continuous babe-scan.

Mirza says, "You still seeing Emina?" His father has stopped mentioning the girlfriend.

"She hit me. With a pot. Right off the stove. Fuck no, I don't see her."

"Why'd she hit you?"

"We were talking about her son. I don't know what I said. The kid is half Serb. She considered, you know, terminating him, way back."

"You mean he's a war kid?"

His father glances at him: "Not that. Her ex went Draža on her. The boy is just ten years old, and he went out on some hunting weekend with his father's Chetnik buddies." Adem stares at his empty bottle: "One more, yes?"

At the apartment Adem sets two shot glasses on the kitchen table and takes out a bottle of brandy. It is exactly as in the war, same pot-bellied little glasses, same cheap slivovitz clear as vodka, except back then there was just one glass on the table.

"Dad, I've had enough."

Adem is pouring the brandy. "Listen to me. You should have it." He fills the glasses and sits, raises his for a toast, waits. Mirza sits opposite and they clink. His father says, "To Bosnia," and they drink, and Adem immediately refills the glasses.

"Dad ..." Mirza smiles uneasily. "Why are you doing this?"

Adem raises his glass.

They have more rounds in silence. Adem begins to pause a few minutes before each refill, blinking slowly at the tabletop. Mirza feels the obliterating warmth come over him. He observes his father's face, the deeply tanned forehead, thick grey-flecked hair, the strong nose with the football-earned bump. Adem blinks away his thoughts and reaches for the bottle, pours with elaborate care. He drinks. Mirza stares at his own full glass. He reaches for it, holds it a moment, drinks it down. His father rises from his chair, takes the bottle, and leaves the kitchen.

They are on the sofa. His father's arm is slung around his neck, their heads touching. Then Adem is on the floor on his back, singing-shouting. The melody seems familiar, something Communist, from football matches or maybe from the war, the war before the war that Mirza knows. There is some banging. Then it comes louder on the apartment door with shouts to shut the fuck up. Adem sings even louder and then he shuts up. The brandy bottle is on its side on the floor. Mirza gets up and goes for it, and his father grips him by the arm and pulls him over, and they are lying side by side. His father is singing again. Mirza doesn't know the tune, but then another one they are both together on, bellowing it out, ignoring the renewed banging from the neighbours.

Mirza wakes up on the floor of his bedroom to the smell of frying sausage. Daylight floods in through the window. Though his head is dully throbbing, he still has some of the happy-vague feeling, the sense that it's all wonderfully pointless and nothing matters. As he staggers out, he sees Adem moving around the kitchen. Mirza closes himself in the toilet and pukes efficiently and feels immediately better even though it briefly enhances the headache. He goes back to bed, his father calling to him about sausage.

Hours later he comes into the kitchen, and Adem is standing staring into the open fridge with a bottle of beer in his hand. He reaches in and takes out another bottle and extends it to Mirza.

"I can't."

"You will feel better."

"Are we going to Makarska?"

Adem straightens up and sticks a palm flat to his forehead. The drama of it indicates sarcasm: "Makarska!" He closes the fridge door, sits at the table. He gestures at Mirza with his beer bottle: "Sit." Mirza sits. His father stares levelly at him. "Did you hear? I shot Ćelo." He plunks his beer on the table and stares hard at it. "Not personally. I arranged it, with some others."

Mirza processes the words. Ćelo was murdered maybe half a year ago. It was headline news in Bosnia. "You said Ćelo was a friend, a business friend."

"Fuck. Friend? No. He was someone I knew."

"Why did you shoot him?"

"He killed people." Adem takes a slug of beer. "And he hurt your mother. And many others. Probably raped guys too."

His father stares straight at him, nodding slowly. Mirza's headache comes back. It's centred like a knifepoint right in the crease between his eyes. He feels like he can't breathe. He's looking at his father's hand around the beer bottle. The nails are dirty. So his mother was raped in Grbavica. That's what happened. The possibility had crossed his mind.

He looks up and into his father's eyes: "In Grbavica."

"Not in. After. Because she went there. Because she was my wife. Because they could pretend she was spying for Serbs." Adem shrugs. "Usual because."

Mirza looks around the room. It doesn't help. Her pots still hang on the wall. Her chair is there. He can touch it. He gave her a piece of chocolate or something while she sat there, a handout from a UN soldier that he'd been saving. He wanted to cheer her up. She sat there staring as if her mind had gone missing. She still does it, sometimes, in Toronto. Fuck-all the UN did to save anyone. They even did business with Ćelo.

His father is speaking: "This is private. You and me only."

"When did she tell you?"

"I knew. She never wanted to talk about it. Then she joined that woman's group in Toronto, at COSTI, so, you know, I think it helped."

Mirza begins to cry. He holds his face firm, but the tears leak out and run down his cheeks. His father watches him calmly. This is the thing they kept quiet about, to "protect" him.

"You should have told me."

"When you were twelve? Thirteen? No. Anyway, you've been told. So now it's your secret too. You have to keep it from her, understood?"

Adem lights a cigarette and inhales deeply, gazing at Mirza, it seems, coldly. He stands and comes behind his son. Mirza feels the strong hand grip his shoulder, then his father's lips touch the top of his head. Adem leaves the room, and Mirza can hear him pissing, the stream steady and forceful as ever. He returns and opens the fridge and takes out another beer, saying, "Don't mention anything about me and Ćelo. Some people know, but don't brag about it. It's better, okay?"

17

They are at Željo's again, Mirza and Kemo and the post-prayer regulars, joined this time by the irregular Damir. The sun's heat presses on them through the canopy over the tables. Damir is due in a month to start his final year at the university in Tuzla, studying chemistry. There is some discussion about the dire job situation in Bosnia, Damir saying there will be jobs coming available at new water treatment and power plants, still in the planning stages. The others think him too optimistic.

As the group breaks up, Mirza tosses in that he'd be happy to give Damir a ride to Tuzla — he will have to drive there for his father anyway. It leads to the two of them chatting while Kemo and the others head for the tram stop, their destination the suburban King Fahd Mosque for some event that doesn't seem to interest Damir. Like Mirza, he didn't join the others at prayers that afternoon, arriving later to meet them at the café.

As they head off through Baščaršija together, Mirza ventures, "You had to miss mosque today?"

"I don't go all the time. And you?"

"I don't go in Canada. Why would I start here?"

"Bad boy."

"Totally."

"So you don't believe?"

"A complicated question."

"Not really. You just answered it."

"Do you believe?"

Damir glances at him. "In Allah, yes. Imams? Not too many. Not at King Fahd anyway."

"What's happening there tonight?"

"I think it's about the guy in jail who might be deported. Mujahedin leader."

Mirza's father knows some of these jailed fighters, mainly Arabs, who joined the war to defend Muslim Bosnia. Some people claimed, and still do, that they were jihadists, imported with the blessing of President Izetbegović. Adem complains about how the arrests are really about pandering to the West to get Bosnia into the EU. Other times he grumbles about extremists and Saudi money lavished on grandiose mosques like the King Fahd.

Damir asks Mirza if he'd like to go for beer or coffee somewhere. Then he's talking on the phone, walking away. He stands under a shop canopy, suddenly in vigorous conversation, as if someone is making absurd demands he refuses to meet. He rejoins Mirza with a slightly sheepish air: "My mother."

Damir turns them into a narrow lane. "Come, we can go to Višegrad. Not the town, a restaurant. Just here."

At Višegrad café there are a few older men drinking coffee out front. Inside, a group at a long table is in the midst of a boisterous meal. Mirza and Damir pull up some chairs outside. Damir has been glancing at his phone and now thumbs in a long message.

"Sorry. My uncle. He knows your father. You're doing some work in Dobrun, yes?"

"Near Dobrun, yeah. The monastery. Not construction. I just delivered some supplies."

"I think my uncle Avdo will come here and you can meet him."

"How does he know my dad?"

"Long time. Since Olympic days." Damir sits back and observes Mirza. "I don't like King Fahd Mosque much, maybe you guessed. One thing, the imam really hates Jews. And Serbs, of course."

"You don't hate Serbs?"

Damir cracks a crooked smile. "I hate Serbs. It's true. I don't hate every Serb. I *suspect* every Serb."

"Kemo told me you were at Srebrenica."

"I was there, yes, at Potočari camp. The battery factory. Višegrad was worse for us, for my family."

"You lost some cousins, Kemo said."

Damir stares at him for a long moment. "Why are we talking about it?"

"We don't have to."

"It's okay. You just — talk like a reporter or something."

"I'm not."

"Your American voice, maybe."

"Canadian."

Damir shrugs. "For us, it's the same."

"It's not the same at all. It's like saying Bosnia and Serbia are the same."

"I only mean the accent. Not the country."

The diners inside are singing, some *sevdah* tune Mirza recalls from childhood.

Damir is watching him: "So you are completely Canadian now?"

"No. Not at all."

"You are here to be Bosnian again?"

"I guess I am, yeah. I'd like to figure out what happened."

"Start with all the leaders and go down the list."

A harried-looking waitress comes and takes their beer order. Inside, the dinner group is singing something about the old Mostar bridge. It crosses Mirza's mind that they should really be singing about the old Višegrad bridge. The joined voices are imperfect and passionate, drifting out into the narrow street.

Mirza says, "Do you visit the graveyard in Potočari, the memorial?"

"You are doing it again, Mr. CNN." But Damir

looks unruffled. "My cousins are not at Potočari. Their bones are still out in the woods somewhere."

"I'm sorry."

"You are not the one to be sorry."

Mirza nods. After a moment he says, "My grandpa was wounded — his head."

"Yes. I remember him."

"My father got shot too, but not so bad."

"That is clear."

"And my mother was —" Mirza stops.

"And mine."

"I don't mean we had it as bad as you."

"I know. It doesn't matter."

"I'm working on something related to Bosnia, some work for a show in Toronto."

"Kemo told me. You are an artist."

"It's political. But I'm not putting any flags on it."

"Okay."

"You could call it anti-war. Kind of like *Guernica*. In spirit at least. You know it? A painting."

"Picasso. Horses."

"Yes, horses, people, screaming."

"A mother and a baby."

"Yes. Mine is an installation, human figures."

Damir watches his face: "You want to come back to all that?"

"Don't you come back to it, every day?"

"I would not say every day."

"I don't believe you."

"I would like it not to be every day. Maybe you want it."

The waitress comes with their beer. They touch bottlenecks and drink.

A little later, the uncle joins them, greeting the men at the next table. He catches the waitress's eye and mimes that he wants coffee, then drops into the chair beside Mirza.

"Do you remember me?" Mirza doesn't. "Avdo. I had some dealings with Adem way back, the boom time, Olympics and after. I saw you as a little guy, you were three or four. So, you are working for Papa. No jobs in Canada?"

"I'm here for now. Just reconnecting."

"Plan to stay?"

"Maybe."

"You with your dad in Kovači?"

"Same apartment. Right next to Damir's, used to be."

"I moved them into that ruin. Your grandpa got a piece of that shell, yes? Or another one. Serbs didn't mind killing their own grandpas then."

Avdo's dark-rimmed eyes swivel to the men nearby. "Gentlemen! We have an Osmanović here. Adem's son." The four eye Mirza. "Your father is making a new name for himself. I mean, aside from his love affair with Ćelo..." Damir snorts at this. The others seem in on the joke too. "Good riddance to that killer." Avdo sits back and looks Mirza up and down. "Your father is a hero."

"He doesn't want to be."

"Hero all round. The police would give him a medal if they could. Nobody liked Ćelo, only feared him. I have done a lot of work for your father. Last few months. I poured the foundation in Visoko. Things have stalled with the pyramids, I regret."

Mirza says, "I was there with my dad last week. The loader was gone."

"We need the loader somewhere else." Avdo looks squarely at him. "Your father has lost some allies, Mirza. He is selling to some Serb guys in RS. I do it too. But you have to choose your friends. Your dad misjudged, selling roofing tiles to Domoševa monastery."

"To monks?"

Damir picks at his beer label: "It's not about the monks."

Avdo's Turkish coffee arrives. He loads sugar into the pot and gently swirls it. Looking at his sallow face, the purple circles under his eyes, Mirza thinks he must put away dangerous amounts of caffeine.

"The monks, pah, I don't care. But the abbot. Arsenije. The holy father. I know what Adem thinks, that we should just try to do business, move things to present time. I understand, but justice has never been done with this guy. He is pure-blood Chetnik. He should be wearing a fur hat. Do you mind if I smoke?" Avdo takes out his pack of Drinas. "I only ask because you are Canadian."

"You don't need to ask."

"Have you heard of Milan Lukić?" Mirza nods. Everyone knows Lukić, the butcher of Višegrad. "And do you know where did Lukić go to have his crimes blessed? To Arsenije. At Domoševa. Now Milan is at the Hague Tribunal. Maybe you watch him on TV."

"No."

"Just as well. He might make you sick." He tips coffee carefully into his demitasse. "I remember Milan from school. I was graduating when he came in. He was a weedy little snot of a kid, but he made a lot of noise. Milan Lukić threw my father off the Višegrad bridge. He beat him first. We don't know if he died on the bridge or in the river. For my brother and his son, he locked them inside a house and burned it. Along with about seventy others, I have to say. This is not to mention all the other killings, and the women he tortured in Vilina Vlas." Avdo lifts his cup slowly and sips, places it delicately back in the saucer. "I say this only because your father should know who he is selling to. I assume he doesn't know, though it's hard to see how he couldn't. He is not making an effort to know. He's only trying to do business. But this is why Visoko is stalled. His workers, his suppliers, too many came from those Drina villages. Of course, Visoko is also stalled for other reasons, mainly because the pyramids are bullshit. Are you boys hungry?"

"We ate after mosque," says Damir.

Avdo gets up and goes inside. Mirza is thinking there's another delivery he's due to make in a few days, to an address in the same part of Republika Srpska.

Damir is faintly smiling: "Are you feeling more Bosnian now?"

"How can I possibly be more Bosnian?"

"You are right."

"And I'm also mixed family. Not like you."

"I don't want to compare."

"My father hates these divisions. He must be ignorant about this abbot."

"Everybody knows."

"If he knows, he is willing to move on from it."

"Move on from what? Did Lukić kill your family?"

"He didn't have dealings with Lukić. So this abbot blessed killers. How many rapists and killers got a blessing from their imams? My father does business with mosques too."

Mirza's heart is pumping. The men at the other table are looking at him and Damir as if watching a football game on TV but only a mildly interesting one. Avdo comes back with a slab of meat *burek* on a plate. As they sit in silence he forks the food into his mouth. A question has formed in Mirza's mind, and his heart pumps even harder as he speaks it.

"Do you do business only with innocent people?"

Avdo finishes chewing and swallowing. "Impossible. It's a question of degrees."

"But everyone did business with Ćelo, yes?"

"There was an incentive, self-preservation. That is not a factor with our Chetnik abbot."

"Why don't you talk to my father yourself?"

"I did. He almost tore my ears off."

"You want him to tear mine off?"

"Why not? He's your father."

PART THREE

18

I've had a message from my nephew. The MOCCA gallery wants Mirza for the October showcase. He's in. Mirza has asked me to get the studio key to his agent, who wants to consider whether a piece or two might be shown in her own gallery in advance of the group show. The agent, Lydia Rajak, suggests we meet at Mirza's studio; she wants me there to "give a context" to the artist and the work.

We meet in the lobby of the building on King West. As we stand together awaiting the elevator, she wafts a spicy nasturtium scent, more intense as we ascend in the cramped cubicle. She hands me her card: NOVA VAROS ART.

I unlock the door and motion her in ahead of me. She stands barely inside the entrance and takes in the array of mangled figures. Two of them, women, are clothed now, if mud- and blood-caked scraps of cocktail dress can be called clothing. The mutilation, the shock of it, is surprisingly convincing. Mirza has been hard at work. Lydia's face is unreadable. She moves closer, then suddenly breathes in deeply through her nose and releases it in a long sigh.

"May I ask, was Mirza, as a child, directly affected by this sort of atrocity?"

"He hasn't discussed it much, until recently. He did spend the entire siege in Sarajevo."

"And you?"

"I've never lived in Bosnia. I helped them settle here after the war."

"Them."

"Him and his parents."

"When was that?"

"Nineteen ninety-six. He was thirteen."

"He hasn't mentioned his parents. Only you."

"We seem to have a good rapport."

"You're a supporter. That's how he put it."

"He hasn't had much support from family, not for this."

Lydia is digging through her bag. "I'll just take some pictures." She moves around the room, aiming her phone.

I glance again at her card. "Are you from Nova Varos? It's in Serbia, isn't it?"

"It is, though I'm actually from Valjevo. I've been here twenty-five years. My mother's parents are from Nova Varos. They still live there."

"What do you think of the work?"

Lydia eyeballs me. "Well, that discussion is, I suppose, for me and Mirza. But I think it's bound to create a stir. This takes us right back to Mark Prent, updates him in fact. But I like the refusal of realism." She scans the figures. "I mean, there's a real narrative in this, an explicit one, unlike Prent, but the representation, well, the horror of it is just unreal enough. It's not about voyeurism. There's anger, but it's, hmm — sardonic, a horrible joke but completely serious. That the end point of all the ethnic cleansing, massacres, the UN thing, peacekeepers, is this obscene punchline in the halls of diplomacy: an exhumation cocktail party. It's got the drama of epic theatre, if you think about it. Of Brecht."

"I see. If not quite Brecht's humour. I'm a little worried about the darkness of it, where it will lead him, and why it's taken so long to surface. His mother is appalled by all this, actually."

"What's he doing in Bosnia?"

"I'm not quite sure. Research, he says. And some construction-type work with his father."

"Well, this should bring him back."

"Do you normally deal in this kind of thing?"

"What? Installations?"

"I mean this level of, I don't know, in-your-face politicized art. I wonder if people will actually want it in their homes."

"Depends on the people. And their homes. Or who they work for, of course. Who they buy for."

19

Kristina arrives as arranged, bearing a bottle of Chilean white. I've made a gazpacho. We start off in the garden but after a few minutes are driven back inside by a children's pool party next door. I check on our father, who is asleep in the TV room, and we resettle at the island in the kitchen. Krista says she has heard from Adem. He advises that our Makarska holiday should be March or April, before the rental season begins.

"Maybe April," I say, "for the weather."

"It'll be like May or June here."

"Wonderful. A proper family holiday."

Krista spoons her soup tentatively, as if the food can't quite be trusted even though it gives her pleasure.

"I don't know if Mirza told you, but I met with his agent. She wants to preview his work at her gallery, before the group show."

"Group show?"

"At MOCCA, on Queen West. He hasn't told you?

"He tells me nothing."

"It's all set. Late October."

"This would be the hacked-up clothes dummies, yes?"

"Do you think of them like that?"

"That's what I see."

"They're different now. More real. More disturbing actually."

"Lovely."

"It's quite a break for him. He'll get media attention."

"I'm glad for that. But I think he's too obsessed to consider how it affects people."

"That's how real artists work, isn't it? Maybe you're just too close to the issues, to him."

"Too close. What does that mean? I'm as close as I am." She sighs and turns toward the window, the faint cries of the neighbour children. "It's good he's finally getting some notice."

"You might tell him that. Just to break the chill a little. He doesn't actually *intend* to upset you."

"We upset each other. It's become a reflex." Krista stares out the window. "We should have got him into counselling, years ago. That's what led to this. He thinks of me as part of the problem. That's why he's gone back there."

"Krista, honestly, he's beyond that. He's not there as a reaction to you. In a way, he's there *for you*. Your objections are just an irritant."

"Is that supposed to comfort me?"

"You did hack his email."

"Do you know what a hack is, Alex? I did not 'hack.' He left it sitting there, waiting."

"Waiting for his mother to snoop?"

"Easier than talking to me."

"I suspect that you not talking to each other for a while could actually help things."

"Maybe. Being with Adem day in and day out will definitely not."

"I guess he has to find that out himself."

"It's the context that concerns me. Reopening stuff, all the bad stuff, just because they're both there."

I hesitate. "What stuff? Daddy's injury?"

"No. That's always been open. And I think we need to change the subject now." Her eyes hold on me for just a moment, a pleading. "All right?"

"All right. Yes."

Krista takes a spoonful of soup, and it seems like an effort to normalize. The tasting, the swallowing. Then she places the spoon squarely on her saucer, as if completing a task.

"Have some bread."

She gives the baguette a remote look. I concentrate on my soup, watching her gaze drift to other places. I say, mildly upbeat, "In any case, Mirza will be back soon enough. To prepare for the show."

"Who's paying for these plane tickets? Not

Adem." Krista's combative tone has come back.

"He got a grant."

"You see? I know nothing."

I'm trying to eat slowly, somewhat closer to my sister's pace, but it's obvious now that she's done, her bowl still half full. I finish and get up to clear things.

"Would you like a sweet? I've got baklava."

"Go ahead, I'm fine."

I refresh Krista's wine and leave the bottle for her.

"Did Adem say he'll join us in Makarska? Krista?"

"Um, yes. That's the plan."

"We must get him to commit. The more Daddy sees us there, the familiar faces, the context, the more he might link things, recall things from those summers. We have to remember to bring the wedding photos, all the holiday pictures from childhood on. From Southampton too."

"There may be some of those still in Kovači. Maybe Mirza can find them. I don't know why we didn't try this years ago. It's bound to help him."

"It will help all of us."

The pool party children are gone. We've moved back outdoors, I with my baklava, and Krista with her wine. I watch her eyes scan over the garden.

"Your roses are always stunning. How do you keep the aphids away?"

"Chemicals."

"We never really made a garden. Adem just wanted edibles, peppers and tomatoes."

"And your rhubarb."

"He didn't even know what that was. Too English."

We sit quietly. Krista's worry lines seem to be easing.

She says, "You know, I can't say I've missed Adem. It simplifies things in one way. We weren't talking — only the most banal required stuff. Now we simply can't talk. I actually think I don't want him in the house again." She looks at me matter-of-factly, then takes a hit of wine, as if rounding off the thought.

"There's always the phone."

"He won't give his number. And if I call the apartment, it just rings."

We both settle into our thoughts. The afternoon is a gift, the air gentle and scented. A bee skims over the window boxes, then comes to dart and hover above Krista's glass. It tries to light on the rim, and she shoos it away, then we watch it settle to feast on the honey trail left on my plate. Krista glances at me. For a moment her whole face is a soft smile. Our father kept bees for a while at Southampton. It always amused us when people panicked and swatted at them and *then* got stung.

I ask Krista, "Did you ever look at Daddy's memoir?"

"The thing about the Youth Brigades?"

"His manuscript, the one you got copied."

"I never read it till he moved to Sarajevo."

"I wish now he'd written it in English."

"Your Serbian's that rusty?"

"I never actually learned it, certainly not for reading."

"We spoke it every day at home."

"No we didn't. They talked to us in English."

"Oh, Alex, they spoke Serbian all the time."

"To each other."

"And to us!"

"Rarely. If they were upset about something. You're misremembering."

"You can't read Daddy's memoir?"

"I struggled through a page or two at your place, years ago."

"Maybe you just need a dictionary?"

"Krista, I'd need a course. Why would I be even close to a reading level? You're the one who lived there for fifteen years."

She stares at me, slack-jawed. "Huh," she says.

"So what's the memoir about?"

"It's — well, it's not about the war. I mean that's in it, but it's really the Tito Youth thing."

"Brotherhood and Unity."

"Exactly. Rebuilding. Daddy helped build Koševo Stadium."

"The Olympic stadium?"

"Same one. They just spruced it up for the Olympics. He saw Tito speak there, telling them to build more stuff. So they all went out and did it, boys and girls together. Highways, railway tunnels ... That long scar on his leg? He was dragged by a horse."

"I knew that."

"Oh yes, it's full of drama. He connected with some of these old guys when he came back to live with us. He used to go and have coffee with them, before everything went to hell. Šaban especially. Šaban and his wife came to the apartment sometimes. Šaban had a big dent in his head. From a shovel or something, not from the war."

"Did Mirza ever read the memoir?"

"He read it with me and Daddy, before the shelling, before Daddy got hurt. I was looking for things Mirza could study at home. We made it like a lesson. I had the idea he could recite from the manuscript aloud, if people came over. He used to rehearse it for us. That's actually when Adem most connected with Daddy, when they got talking about Tito and their Communist fathers, grandfathers, the whole thing. Then after, sometime after Daddy's injury, Mirza gave a reading. That summer, ninety-four, we had almost no shelling. We even had water and power sometimes. People were visiting, the trams were running. We invited Amila and Ismet over with their kids, and Mirza read aloud. He read it beautifully, made it like a drama. Adem brought out the brandy, the *domaća* stuff from his brother. It was like Partisans' homecoming week because Daddy — well, all we heard from him day after day was this stuff, and we just tuned it out. But with friends there and people remembering the old days, it was a party. We almost felt like the war was over."

After Kristina leaves, I set up my father in the backyard with the old holiday album. I watch him now from the kitchen window, dozing with his weathered face tilted to the sun. The plans for Makarska are giving me a needed boost. Krista and I have already begun mentioning to Pero what's in store. Though he loses the thought minutes later, the idea of a seaside family holiday always puts a little extra light in his eyes. I present it as a trip "home." If he mentions Sarajevo, I quickly correct, "No, even better: our summertime home!" Then the photos come out, himself and me and Mother and Krista, backdropped by beach and blue water — a connection to better times in a place that managed to avoid the destruction.

Makarska and its setting are the map of my childhood summers. The same, of course, is true for Mirza. I might have made more of an effort to visit in those years. I watched Mirza grow up in snapshots sent through the mail. I haven't been to

Makarska since the time of Krista's wedding, but I recall Adem's family house being much like the one our parents rented each year just up the hill: full of sunlight and sea breezes. Adem says not much has changed in the town aside from some beachfront expansion, limited by the horseshoe bay and craggy hills.

I will take my full four weeks from the library. My father will walk through the old streets with me, with his daughter, with his nephew, looking out at the familiar arc of shoreline. It's bound to be a restorative for Kristina and for Mirza too, something to pull them out of bad memories. Mirza's show at the gallery will come and go. It might even be a kind of exorcism for him.

My father now appears to be staring fiercely at me from his chair in the yard, but I know he can't see me, here behind the glass in the dim house. He has these stare episodes, seeing things that aren't actually present, as we all do. But while the rest of us stare at the past with some detachment, maybe a reassessing, Pero simply relives it. I can see it in him now, the emotions stirring. He might start yelling. He clutches the arms of his chair. Yes, here it comes.

"Cunt of your mother!"

The words penetrate two panes of glass. Fortunately, they are not in English. I get out of my chair as I see him rise from his. We meet as we both try to go through the screen door. He shoulders past me, through the porch and into the kitchen, where he stops. He looks around, jaw working, his eyes shifting.

"Are you hungry, *Tata*?"

He glares at me.

"Maybe a snack? A banana? Oatmeal cookie? They're nice and soft."

He stares through the kitchen window as if the outrage might still be out there, stalking him. He sits slowly at the table. His anger is draining.

"Have a cookie and some cold milk — or a coffee?"

"A banana. Thank you. And milk."

20

Sarajevo had been so quiet, for days. Pero was thinking he might even take his grandson with him. It was a pleasant dream of a thought, banished completely when Kristina came back from her outing. He had his jacket on and was just having a last-minute pee, thinking how much Mirza had enjoyed his previous visit to Šaban's house. It was shortly before the shootings outside the church. Snow was still in the streets then. Alma had made walnut pastries, and they watched a football game.

Now he was thinking only of renewing the boy's pleasure, but Krista's presence brought along her motherly authority. Mirza stayed home, and Pero went alone to see his old friend, a little defiantly, shrugging off his daughter's worries of risk. He could, he said, be just as easily run down by a tram.

Šaban and Alma were in Logavina Street, almost at the top by the old orphanage. Pero was beginning the climb up the block rising steeply from the tramline when he heard a whistle in the air above his head and a moment later an explosion somewhere far up the hill. He stopped in the entryway of a shop and stared up the narrow street as shouts began to drift down. A plume of smoke rolled up over the rooftops. A half block away the police station disgorged a handful of officers. They searched the sky and began to sprint up the street. A cruiser tore past them. Pero stood for long moments wondering what to do. He decided he had to know if Šaban and his wife were safe.

As he came up the street to the primary school another shell came in. The blast hit him like a wall. He returned to his senses lying flat on his back. He rolled onto his side and managed to get up on all fours, then slowly to his feet. His head was ringing. Chunks of brick and tile were strewn across the schoolyard. When he looked up he saw a huge bite out of the corner of the schoolhouse roof. Dust hung in the air and caught in his throat. Pain began to shoot through his right arm. He could see a rip in the cloth of his jacket. He moved to the steps near the school doors and sat. In a daze he observed people passing him, going in and out of the school. A car sped down the street with limbs poking out of its open tailgate. Behind a row of shrubs nearby two men were staring at the ground. A young man stopped before him.

"Are you okay, sir?"

"My arm."

"Here, take your jacket off. Let me ..."

Pero's shirt sleeve was bloody. The man rolled

up the sleeve. There was a small puncture in the fleshy part of Pero's arm just below the elbow. A line of blood ran down, dripping onto the concrete steps.

"You'll be all right. Does it hurt?"

"Yes. Not badly. I'm lucky."

"I think you must keep your hand pressed to it."

"Yes. My daughter will patch me up."

"Go into the school. The shelter, in case ..."

"Thank you."

The young man went on up the street.

Pero sat in the school cellar with women and children and old people. A woman, a teacher, told him they had just resumed some classes in the basement shelter. Now they would stop. The woman looked at his arm. She returned with some disinfectant and scissors, and she cut off his bloody shirt sleeve and tied his handkerchief tight against the wound. The pain was worse now, but there seemed to be less blood. His arm and hand were functional. He had indeed been lucky.

He waited until it seemed there would not be more shells. A half hour had gone by when he trudged back up to the street. He could hear a woman wailing nearby. Passing the hedge at the end of the schoolyard he came upon the weeping woman and a body under a blanket. Blood was pooled in the dirt. He stared at her fingers touching the blanket, pulling away. He carried on up the street with the woman's sobs chasing him.

When he came to Šaban and Alma's house all seemed intact, and when he knocked they were inside. Alma was in tears. The first shell had crashed through the roof of a house just up the street. The news was that three had been killed and others injured, including two children. Two of the dead were the mother and grandmother. They had known the family for twenty years. Alma said she would look at Pero's wound, but he told them it was taken care of at the school. He was able to add that he seemed to be the only injured one inside the shelter.

Alma made some coffee, and they sat and tried to make sense of things, of what was to be expected, whether they could even continue to live in their own streets. Alma's silent tears never stopped all through their conversation. Pero eventually checked his watch. He realized he had to go home. The shelling would be on the news, and his daughter would be worried. Alma thought Pero should stop by at the doctor's office down near the police station.

Šaban said, "What do you mean? The doctor will be out where he's needed."

"It's worth a try," Alma snapped at him, and Šaban shrugged in acquiescence.

Pero did stop later at the doctor's and found a woman and child waiting in the entranceway. He began the walk back to the apartment. As he came up the street Kristina's voice rang out. She was leaning from a window.

"Are you all right? It's been almost three hours, *Tata*!"

"I'm fine! Everything's fine!"

"You don't look good!"

"I'm fine! Šaban and Alma are also fine!"

"Their street was hit!"

"Hit! Yes! Now stop shouting!"

The walk home had made him aware of his sore body. He'd been thrown to the pavement. He was lucky he didn't have broken bones or a cracked head. Of course Krista knew at a glance that he'd been hurt. When he took off his jacket in the apartment, she stared at the bloody handkerchief on his arm and told him he simply could not go out anymore. This, on top of the pain, he did not need.

"I should be cooped up here like an invalid?"

"What, you will risk your life only to go visiting? And you wanted to take Mirza!"

He might have killed his grandson. The child stood now not three paces from him. The thought was overwhelming.

"I visit my friends. I will not stop. And how many times have I returned with food as well, yes? Enough! Why should you take the only risk, Krista? You are dispensable?"

Kristina gaped at him, then the tears came.

21

My father said that Sarajevans were the real Yugoslavs of Yugoslavia. Like his parents, he put collective identity ahead of any idea of religion or blood — Serb or Croat or anything else. My mother remained more defensively Serbian, having been turfed from her Zagreb home by murderous Croats. But I never thought of myself as a Serb or a Yugoslav. Raised to be as English as my parents could accomplish without disparaging our heritage, I was more than happy to ignore that heritage completely. Only on summer holidays was the old country gently imposed on me and my sister. When Kristina fell for Adem in Makarska, that's when she began to be a Yugoslav — and then, decidedly, a Sarajevan.

Lyle only made me more British. I met him in that most English of settings, the Victoria and Albert Museum. I entered the gallery containing the towering plaster knock-off of Michelangelo's *David* and found Lyle at its feet. His fingers were resting shyly on David's massive toes. I watched his gaze move slowly up the length of pale, naked limbs, then he glanced at me. That was that. We had tea in the café. He was a doctor, a just-certified endocrinologist. (I learned the word that day.) I was still at London University. We exchanged numbers and met later for dinner. A few years on, he was accepted to a hospital posting in Canada, and we began the process of finding a way for me to join him. If it were now, I simply could have married him.

For most of one summer in Makarska, I put up with a sister who would not shut up about the handsome, amusing, heaven-sent Adem, the Adem who seemed to be in the house every day and for too many family dinners. He was a few years older. He talked about the instant money that would be made when Sarajevo snagged the Olympics. There was some initial parental consternation about Adem and Kristina, but a year or so later they were married and she was off to a life in Sarajevo. Then my parents had to deal with Lyle, but not for long.

When I disappeared with Lyle to Toronto, I began years of giving hardly a thought to Yugoslavia, interrupted only by our Olympic-year visit. I remember our last day there. Adem drove us into the mountains in his aging Mercedes, the packed car labouring up the steep grades. Mirza was just a toddler. It was the last time the family was all together before my mother died. Adem stopped and made us get out to stare across a snowy field at a monument to dead Partisans: a gigantic brutalist flower with concrete petals like broken wings. My father told us his Brigade cohort had gathered up the bones of Partisan heroes right on that very spot. They took them away and buried them in a proper cemetery. They had found German dead too, but they left them. We stood there trying to imagine the scene Pero had in his head. Then the icy wind forced us all back into the car.

Adem's brother Medo, also a soldier, died in the same month I lost Lyle: July 1995. He'd been part of the effort that summer to defend Srebrenica. Sitting on my porch one night with Adem, maybe a month after they arrived, I asked him about his brother and heard more than I'd wanted to. Medo's body lay in a ditch with two others for days while the Serbs blocked access, occasionally firing bullets into the corpses. Then the bodies disappeared to no one knows where. I've been told there is no grave site, just a stone marker in a nearby village with Medo's and other names on it.

When I got Kristina's call about Adem's brother, and about the subsequent massacre of thousands that was just appearing in the news reports, my letter to her about Lyle had only just been posted. It was the strangest conversation. In the numbed inflections I'd come to know, Kristina told me of

Medo's death and the ensuing mass killings. Then I told her about Lyle — which oddly triggered her dissolution into sobs. I got my story out: the accident, the hospital, the nothing-they-could-do. Then it seemed neither of us had words, only tears. We muttered our love and goodbyes.

I put the phone down. The world around me came in through my eyes. There it was: my living room, my furniture, the hum of the air conditioner, my forearms and hands resting on the arms of the chair, the presence of my flesh, its weight, the flesh and bone called Alex. Outside the window were trees and sky and neighbours' houses. It was all there as usual. And absolutely everything was without significance except in one aspect. Everything my eyes took in seemed a cause of pain, even the leaves on the trees.

Accident is a synonym for failure to identify causes. Lyle's killer, Penny Giakoumis, did not set out in her car with murderous intent. But the outcome was the same. Penny killed Lyle. It was no more an accident than is a death from cancer, AIDS, warfare, or famine. The trial process, which I eventually stopped attending for the sake of sanity, established some causes: fatigue, inattention, weather, speed. Nothing could mitigate the glaring cause: that she drove fully conscious through a perfectly functioning red signal light. She was sentenced, after an appeal trial, to six months in minimum security. In a negotiated settlement with the insurers, I received a pain and suffering amount. Penny's prison facility was essentially a motel with a chain-link fence around it. She could go out every four weeks to spend a weekend with her family and could even go biweekly to the local public library. Fortunately for both of us, it was not the branch I worked in. I would like to forgive her. I can't. Someday, maybe.

22

Mirza's father has sent him back to Višegrad region with a load of lumber and bricks. His destination is a house-building site in Dobrun, the village with the nearby Domoševa monastery and the alleged Chetnik abbot. He has not mentioned anything to his father about his chat with Damir's uncle, about Avdo's critical words. He can't think how to begin a conversation with his father about the connections his Serb clients might have. Doesn't just about everyone doing business here have these connections? Even in the war the opposing sides made business deals.

Driving along the Drina gorge, through the plunging rock cuts and arched highway tunnels he recalls from childhood holidays, he considers the middle ground he occupies. He doesn't suspect every Serb as Damir does, let alone hate Serbs in general. In fact it was Muslim Ćelo he might have truly hated — but Ćelo is gone, executed for his crimes. Knowing now about his mother, what Ćelo did, Mirza finds her popping more into his mind: how she was afterward, the new meaning of it. In the truck now it brings the unwanted prick of tears. He forces them away with a shake of his head.

He concentrates on the familiar landscape, rocky hills rising out of the Drina's blue-green water. He is feeling strangely separate from everything he recognizes. It's like he forgot, for years, to remember these things, as if the good memories, the pre-war ones, got pushed out by all that came after.

There was the day at the brewery with Kemo. They shouldn't have gone there. They knew it, and as if to punish them, sure enough something horrible and unreal happened. He doesn't think about the day at the brewery. What comes is involuntary and has nothing to do with thinking.

He hates the bombers and killers and rapists, all of them, but he condemns almost equally the peace-keepers and their bosses. That's when his blood begins to simmer: when he thinks of the UNPROFOR commander retired now to his Muskoka home with his souvenir pistol from Karadzić. The "peacekeeper" reminiscing about dinners with his mass-killer buddy.

The UN failures were the cause of Mirza's first serious fight with Teo, just after the headline news that one of Karadzić's cronies had been arrested and shipped off to the Hague. They were lounging on the grass by the playing field fence, everything cool until Mirza tensed it up by saying that maybe they should send a few of Karadzić's peacekeeper friends to the Hague too. This time Teo wasn't content with just rolling his eyes. He went from indignant to ballistic. He said Mirza couldn't dilute Serb guilt by dumping it on UN troops. Mirza countered that it was about apportioning guilt, not excusing it. Teo, half Croat, conveniently has no taint of Serbness. This was the never mentioned fact, the moral high ground Teo would have fiercely denied occupying. Maybe Mirza was only imagining that his mother's Serbness mattered in any way to Teo. But the subject couldn't be raised.

There was a similar thing with Kemo too, the way he just went quiet on the rare occasions when Mirza mentioned his mother's visit to Grbavica, her black silences and panic attacks when she came back. His father's position was that they should keep the whole incident within the family, but everyone seemed to know she'd gone there. Mirza may have talked only once or twice about it with Kemo, never with any specifics because he didn't know about the rape then. It seemed at the time a thing that left a gap in conversation, made neighbours shift their eyes and change the subject. Of course, they had their own traumas. But sniper wounds and bombings were always talked about. Neighbours came with food and help. After Kristina and Grbavica, help came, but it often seemed furtive. Food was left anonymously. People asked how she was, but with a formal attitude, almost accusing.

Mirza is approaching a tunnel. He hurtles into the black and kicks up the high beams to almost no effect, he is so sun-blinded. He slows as white masses slide past the truck on the right: sheep escaping the midday heat, drowsing on the narrow shoulder. Sheep and goats and people die in these tunnels, though no one he knows has ever hit an animal and suffered much beyond a mangled fender. Still, entering the void is always a heart-flipping moment. Far ahead, a thumbnail of white light is visible.

There was an incident, a dispute one day on the landing when Mirza's father came home with water. Kemo's older brother was with him. For just a moment the two men were shouting, and then Adem came in red-faced, lugging the jugs. Halid had said something to set him off: *some shit about Grbavica*. Adem banged around in the kitchen. He called Halid a paper mujahedin. *We're not Muslim enough? Fuck him!* Mirza had seen Halid praying when he was home on leave, in the bedroom he shared with Kemo. It was jarring because the Jašarević family had never prayed; they'd always been Titoists and Communists all the way.

Out in the sun again with another tunnel ahead, Mirza is hit with a smack of revelation. The UN pass. The forged pass had come from Halid's friends. It was meant for Adem, to help with the transport of goods and smuggled weapons through the Butmir tunnel. Halid guessed, rightly, that Kristina had used it to get past the checkpoints into Grbavica. It just added more to the paranoid logic, or planted rumour, that she was a spy for the Serbs and whatever happened to her was probably deserved. It explained why Mirza's father claimed urgent business elsewhere the day Halid's bones were buried. But Mirza thinks his friendship with Kemo is still a fact, even if there is a feeling of transition about it. What will Kemo think of all his trucking of supplies to Višegrad, a region known more or less as Chetnik central? But Kemo probably already knows about this from Damir.

He has passed the hydroelectric dam. Another few minutes and he'll be coming down toward the old Turkish bridge, its stone arches vaulting across the Drina to the Višegrad town centre. He has heard more than once that his grandfather helped reconstruct this bridge after the Germans bombed it. Further on, the highway will take Mirza over the Drina on a nondescript steel bridge.

On his last trip, he got turned around somehow by the twists of the river road and completely lost his compass sense, heading north when he thought he was going southeast to Dobrun. Now he comes off the bridge with his north–south instincts again weirdly reversed. He knows he should go left at the T-junction, yet he finds the truck again hugging right. He swears and veers sharply to the left, and there he sees a police car, just as before, sitting outside a deserted *kafana*. Mirza hits the brakes. The truck skids to a stop between lanes in a triangle of disused blacktop. A paunchy officer crosses toward him, waving his little red disc on a stick. Mirza gets out his wallet, and as the officer nears he blurts in Serbian that he doesn't know the area.

"Right, left ... I got confused." He mugs contrition.

"Licence."

Mirza takes out his Ontario driver's licence, which happens to prove him Muslim on two counts: *Mirza* and *Osmanović*.

"Registration."

The cop returns to his VW police cruiser. He sits half in, half out of the car, takes his cap off, scrubs a palm over his head, opens a water bottle and drinks, methodically screws the lid back on. He settles to examining the documents. Mirza knows the truck is registered to his father, which will help legitimatize him. He's thinking he'll get nailed with failing to signal. They seem absurdly vigilant about it here.

The officer puts his cap back on and returns.

"Toronto."

"Yes, sir."

"I have some cousins in Hamilton."

"Yeah, big Serbian community. Bosnian, whatever."

"What have you got back there?" He angles his

head at the cargo, which is perfectly visible: terra cotta brick, wooden planking.

"Construction. I work for my father."

"His name?"

"Adem Osmanović."

"Are you lost?"

"No, sir."

"Do you know where you are?"

"Višegrad. I'm going to Dobrun."

"It's left. Not right."

"I know. Thank you."

"Your father is a builder?"

"I'm just delivering. The builder is local."

"Who is the builder?"

Mirza has the invoice beside him. He gives it to the officer, who scans it and smirks.

"Your father is working for a Chetnik, does he know that?"

"Yes, I think he knows. He's not working for him."

"No? His name is right here."

"Okay."

"You know, your licence is shit. You are driving a commercial vehicle."

"I'm sorry. I'm here only a month or two."

"This is Serbia." The cop jigs his finger up and down in front of his sweaty face, indicating the ground he patrols. "You are in RS here. Not Federation."

"Yes, sir. I know."

"Would you like a beer?"

"A beer? I don't think I can ..."

"You can. It's a hot day. I'm ready for lunch." The cop tilts his head back, assessing Mirza, as if he's now more of a diversion than an irritant. "You can follow my car."

Mirza follows. They are heading for Dobrun. He remembers the twists of the highway and its clusters of new stucco houses, stalled half-built ones, and weed-choked ruins. The policeman drives at the speed limit or below. In fifteen minutes they are passing the Cyrillic entry sign for Dobrun. The cop pulls into a roadside *bife* with tables and red Nektar Beer umbrellas out front. He gets out of his car and watches Mirza manoeuver the truck between geranium-filled planters, the police cruiser, and a tired-looking vintage Mercedes. The officer now has an avuncular grin on his face. Mirza feels like he's in a dream. He can't park without boxing in the Mercedes, but the cop is miming, *It's okay, don't worry.* Then he disappears into the café.

Mirza hovers near the truck. He's thinking this will be all right. The name on the invoice changed things. A tall woman with skin-tight jeans comes out to the concrete patio with coffee for a table of two men. She glances at Mirza with a quick smile and heads back inside as the policeman comes out. He drops his cap on a table and gestures to Mirza.

"Come. Sit."

Mirza does as he's told. The officer looks refreshed. He has splashed his face and slicked his hair back. Mirza catches the faint chopped-onion scent that comes with a man's workday in summer. His father often smells like this now that he's back in the homeland. Deodorant is for after-hours, for dates and social events.

"Are you hungry?"

Mirza shrugs. Acknowledging that he could eat seems wrong. A policeman offering lunch seems absurd.

"Ljubomir, the guy on your invoice, he owns this restaurant. You don't need to worry."

"Okay."

"Yes. It's okay. Forget that your licence is shit. I was joking."

"Okay."

"But you should still get a proper one. To be legal."

"Okay, sir, I will."

"We know who your father is. Understood? Don't say okay." The cop grins. "Ljubo is not here, sadly. He's at the site, the house. That's where your supplies are going."

The tall woman comes out with two beers and a platter of cold meats and cheese.

"This is Jelena." Jelena tosses a smile on her way back inside. "I am Vlado." He offers his hand, crushes Mirza's, then raises his beer bottle. He waits for Mirza to pick up, and they clink, then drink.

It's a quick lunch. Vlado talks about the weather, jokes a little with the men at the other table. He makes phone calls. He polishes off his beer, orders Mirza to eat the last roll of ham, and then they are off. The meal seems to be on the house.

The building site consists of an L-shaped concrete platform on a treeless hillside lot. The view across the gravel road overlooks rolling meadowland and scraps of forest. There is a guy, aged maybe twenty, mixing cement in a wheelbarrow with a shovel.

"Vuk, where is Ljubo?"

"Gone for something."

"Fucking ... Why doesn't he answer his phone? Help this guy unload, will you?"

Vlado sits in his cruiser, talking on his cell and the police radio. The rail-thin, deeply tanned Vuk works with Mirza in silence. They carry the hollow, bulky clay bricks two at a time, stacking them on a corner of the concrete pad. Before they're finished Vlado calls from the car that he has to leave.

"But you should stay. Stay until Ljubo comes."

They watch Vlado drive off.

Vuk says, "Police escort."

Mirza shrugs. "He thought I was lost."

"But you were not."

"No. I've been here before."

"Here?"

"The area."

They finish the unloading, and Vuk asks if Mirza can spare a cigarette.

"I don't smoke."

"What's your name?"

"Miki."

"Vuk."

They shake. Unlike Vlado's hand, Vuk's has nothing to prove. With hardly a thought Mirza has called himself Miki because he knows it will scan as Serb or neutral. Vuk takes a plastic bucket, fills it from a big trough of stagnant water, and splashes some into the cement barrow. He works with all the enthusiasm of a convict in a prison yard.

"Where you from?"

"Sarajevo. And Canada, Toronto."

"You're from Toronto? What you doing in this place?" Vuk's sinewy arms strain at the paste of cement. "I'll go to Toronto and you can work here, what do you say?"

"Perfect. This Ljubomir guy, is he your boss?"

"He's family. And boss, yeah."

"Do you know when he's coming?"

"He's supposed to come with the bricklayer. I don't know when."

Mirza goes to the truck for his phone. A text from his father reminds him to stop at a particular farm market for what he claims are the best eggs.

Mirza will not forget to do this. He sits on the tailgate watching Vuk, looking around at the dry fields, the sky, a house down the road whose naked walls, like half the ones in rural Bosnia, display a chequerboard of cement-spattered terra cotta meant to be stuccoed and painted someday. Laundry stretches from a window to a metal pole. A red plastic tricycle sits on its side in the tall grass. Vuk has dropped his shovel and is approaching.

"Miki! Do you maybe have some water?"

"Of course, yes, in the cab."

Vuk finds the bottle and takes a big gulp. Sweat is streaming on his forehead. He extends the bottle to Mirza, who drinks and passes it back.

"You can finish it. There's more in the truck."

"Thanks. You deliver bricks in Toronto too?"

"Ha. No. I'm just working here for my dad."

"Big Miki."

"No, Adem." Mirza instantly regrets his slip. Vuk tricked him. And Vuk is smiling broadly at him now.

"Adem and Miki "

"Mirza, but really I am called Miki in Toronto."

"You are going back to Toronto, of course."

"I have to, yeah, but I'll be coming back here."

"Why? You are becoming Bosanac? Or maybe soldier for Allah?

"I would pick Bosanac."

"Nice."

"And you?"

"Ah, you know, angry Serb."

"I'm sorry."

"But I was too young to fight." Vuk stares at him stone-faced. Then he grins. He goes back to his wheelbarrow.

Mirza says, "My mother is Serb, if you want to know. She's really pissed that I came back here with my father."

Vuk flashes an elaborate Chetnik salute and resumes turning his cement slop.

"Why does Ljubo want to see me?"

"Because you're the bricks guy? I don't know."

Mirza waits, sitting in the cab with the doors wide open. The scorching air carries no breeze. Vuk is talking on the phone now. He seems to be making arrangements with a friend for the evening. He ends the call and looks at Mirza: "Girlfriend."

"Long-term?"

Vuk laughs. "One month." He sits on the edge of the water trough, thumbing and fingering his phone.

"You can sit here in the truck. It's out of the sun, at least."

Vuk joins him. The two of them focus on their phones. There's a predictable text from Mirza's father, and one from Damir mentioning a party at FIS Kultura, a club he's heard of but not been to. Damir hasn't struck him as a club type. Mirza isn't much a club type lately either, but replying he sees that he's probably ready for a night out. He has spent too many evenings alone Web-crawling; or with his father, falling asleep with the TV on; or at Kemo's talking Islam and Bosnian politics and wondering what his tolerance limit should be for an old friend's religious fervour. But *fervour* is not quite the word. Kemo has an aura of certainty, but he doesn't push it, exactly. Mirza thinks he is probably keeping the real dogma close to his chest, for fear of scaring his old friend. Damir, on the other hand, having said he believes, has since seemed happy to leave religious discussion behind for the complications of regular life — such as which war criminals are too guilty to sell bricks to.

Vuk is now wandering around the site, listlessly shifting objects or just staring vaguely into the distance. Mirza imagines him oppressed by the family bosses, without a plan of escape. But really, Vuk is a mystery.

"Vuk! I can't stay. But I'll be back for sure, at some point."

"I will tell Ljubo."

Mirza starts the truck, then gets out with an unopened bottle of water. He puts it on the concrete pad in the shade of the stacked bricks.

"I don't need that."

"You fucking do in this heat. I can get another."

"Super. See you!"

23

The Sarajevska Pivara is across the river and up the hill from the unrestored ruin of the National Library. Mirza has come for an early dinner with his father in the cavernous restaurant attached to the brewery. They are with one of Adem's construction buddies, Huso, a one-time rock musician. The two men like the place for its view of young female flesh, seen best from the mezzanine tables offering sightlines to almost every corner. The girls baring the most cleavage tend to come with muscled, buzz-topped, hyper-macho males who wear tight T-shirts and expensive jeans and are mostly on their phones while their dates look bored. Mirza's father was in the trenches with some of these men when they were only teenagers and he was ordering them around. Now some of them are his business rivals.

"He's one. There by the bar, with the long-haired blonde. Rizo. A killer. What he did to the Serbs we captured! Yoy! I will not even tell you."

"You can tell me, Dad. What did he do?"

"I can't say. It was not normal."

"What, you mean it was gay?"

"He is just sick in the head. I can't speak for what he does otherwise to get his kicks. Huso, what does he do these days?"

"Sheep. Dogs. I heard he did a chicken."

Adem stares at his friend. "Does he understand no means no?"

"Sheep never say no."

They take swigs from their bottles of Sarajevsko and silently contemplate Rizo.

Huso says, "Look at his whore. She's looking for the exit."

The girl, who could be sixteen, gets up, and Rizo interrupts his phone call to say something to her. She tosses her head and struts away toward the washrooms.

Huso says, "I think she needs to snort something. Who can blame her?" He leans close, his beer-and-cigarette breath washing over Mirza. "Psychopath. The Chetniks were fucking terrified of Rizo. He's on the phone now ordering for some guy to get his knees broken, some Bulgarian who cheated him, whatever. I'm not kidding."

Huso finishes his beer and stands up: "Text me about the Doboj job, okay?"

"You're not eating?"

"I have to drive to Konjic." He puts some cash on the table.

"We'll get it, Hus."

"You fucking will not."

They watch Huso's careful progress down the staircase to the main level. Mirza knows there is some sort of mobility issue, a nerve problem. When Huso goes past Rizo's table, the two men seem to physically acknowledge each other, just barely. They watch him push open the street door.

Adem says, "He shouldn't be driving at all. His reflexes are gone."

His father wants him to take on more responsibility, maybe become a supervisor. This is something Mirza should have anticipated, but all he wants is to continue his undemanding supply runs in the truck while his mind mulls the accumulation of evidence. He hasn't any set idea of what evidence he's gathering but knows that everything he witnesses is relevant, now and for all his future work. Damir and his uncle Avdo, Kemo and his leap to faith, Višegrad and Dobrun, Vlado the cop, Vuk the cement mixer, Rizo the killer — all are part of it. And Srebrenica, regardless of whether he can get Damir to revisit the place, will become more evidence. How it all relates to his actual work, his art, is undefinable. His family is huge a factor, of course. Mirza's work is about his whole life, about everything that has happened. Everything. He doesn't know how to think about this, but he doesn't need to think his life into his work. It will be there.

Adem has long been in the habit of disregarding the artist in his son. Mirza almost never talks art with his father, but right now he needs to punch up the recognition he's getting in Toronto. He also has to book himself time away from the job. This is something they agreed on before Mirza arrived. He especially has to stand firm against any idea of a career in the Bosnian construction industry.

As they came up the hill to the restaurant, Mirza half-listened to his father's rambling monologue about upcoming jobs, plans for the Pyramid Centre, the frustrations of cashflow and bad accounts. Meanwhile, he was peripherally aware of what he was approaching: of what had happened there outside the brewery, with Kemo and the older boy whose name he's forgotten. The memory of it has always come in image flashes, images isolated from the chain of events. But since his return to Sarajevo the insistent presence of the city has reassembled the timeline and what brought them there that day.

The older boy, who they didn't know, passed by in the street with a cart and somehow they ended up joining him and doing the unthinkable: crossing the river to get water from the brewery's onsite well, which had been opened for public access. The brewery was even giving out free plastic jugs. Mirza and Kemo went with him, knowingly breaking a rule in order to increase the general good. They would be punished when they returned home, but the water and jugs would be gratefully put to use.

His father and mother were never told what he and Kemo witnessed that day. They only heard the simpler story that the boys brought home, the one they told only because they were gone so long it was badgered out of them: they went for water, there was a mortar attack, they took shelter, and they came home waterless but without a scratch.

Tonight, before dinner in the same street, Mirza and his father approached the brewery's loading yard with its enclosing brick wall and iron gates. Mirza felt the slow shock of familiarity: the configuration of pavement and brick, the bars and crosspieces of the gates. None of these ordinary sights were significant in themselves. It was the human things they had seen there, thrown up against the wall, mangled and embedded in the bars, when they'd emerged from the building opposite after the shelling stopped.

Their food has come: calamari for Mirza, a pot of goulash for his father. Mirza stares at the black grill marks on the squid, the tangle of crisped tentacles. Adem is tucking into his hot-pot with enthusiasm.

"Do you still remember stuff from the trenches? I mean consciously. Do you think about it?"

"Mirza, let's eat, yes? Do you want another

beer?"

"I'm good."

Adem forks a dripping chunk of beef into his mouth. Through the food he says, "Something specific is bothering you?"

"Just curious."

"I don't recycle the same shit. I've told you, just put it away. I don't know what else to say to you."

"What that guy, down there, did to the Serbs, did it bother you?"

His father stares at him, almost accusatory. Then his gaze shifts, and they are both contemplating Rizo, who is still on the phone.

"If I listed for you all the things that bothered me ... pah, I'm not interested, especially not about Rizo. It's finished. You come here, it brings things back. That's a given. I saw some fucked-up things. What's the point? We have to exist now, not fifteen years ago."

"Okay, you don't have to say more."

"I didn't force you to come, did I? You being here, of course I had to tell you about your mother."

"Yes."

"It was serious. The spying thing, the lies that people fell for. We were in danger after she came back. It's another reason we kept you indoors all the time."

"Well, not all the time."

"Except when you got out, like a fucking stray dog."

Adem reaches over and cuffs Mirza across the head, like he's still a kid. Mirza cuts and eats his squid. It's good, salty and oily and garlicky. This is shaping up into an okay conversation with his father. Sometimes a challenge can make Adem open up, when it doesn't do completely the opposite.

"It makes me think about everything after. How she was. How you were. How people treated us afterwards. That thing with Kemo's brother, and the forged pass."

"Yo-y ... Leave it, Mirza. Leave it." His father freezes and looks directly into Mirza's eyes, not angry, but steady: sending a message. It's a warning, and Mirza knows he should heed it. "So. You were chatting with Avdo, about Dobrun, yes?"

"Yeah."

"But you can't just blindly believe everything."

"I don't, Dad."

"For sure, Avdo is not a terrible guy, but he is not willing to acknowledge that some of his business contacts are just other Ćelos. He doesn't want to hear this complication. Avdo has lost some Serb customers to me. This is his real problem."

"He thinks that priest, the abbot at Dobrun, is a war criminal."

"That's bullshit. He's a nobody." Adem considers Mirza for a long moment, chewing. "Did you know your mother sent me pictures? Of your — I don't know what you call them. Your corpses."

"When?"

"Few months ago."

"They're different now. I have a show coming up."

"I heard."

"It's a real show at a public gallery, on Queen Street. The Museum of Contemporary Canadian Art."

His father stares at him, then raises his beer: "My boy, the Canadian artist."

Mirza feels the smile crack his face, as if the muscles are out of practice. They clink bottlenecks and drink.

His father continues in the same upbeat tone: "You know, just for information, you maybe should watch it with the gay comments."

"What?"

His father lowers his voice: "You ask if Rizo is gay. Okay, it's a joke. For Huso, gay is always a joke, never a serious question. If he thinks it is serious —"

"Dad —"

"Listen to me. He will think I'm back from Canada with a queer son."

"Like it's his business."

"That is what will happen, what they will think. Twice now you have brought it up with Huso."

"I didn't."

"Last time, coming across the bridge, the bar there. You said it was a gay club. How would you even know this?"

"Damir told me."

"If you keep up with it, Huso will only wonder what is Mirza talking about, all this fag stuff ..."

"That is his problem, not mine."

"No. Things are different here. You will lose respect. I will lose respect. I could lose contracts even. There are consequences."

"That's fucked up."

"Welcome to your native land, Mirza." Adem breaks off a chunk of bread and dips it in his stew. "So. Are you?"

"Am I?"

"Are you?" They watch each other. Mirza looks away. "*You are?*"

"I'm ... in the middle."

Mirza continues smoothly eating, trying to keep things light.

His father is staring at the table now. He looks up. "You know, honestly, I am not completely surprised."

"That's good."

"You have spent a lot of time with Alex."

"That is totally not relevant. You think my gay uncle turned me gay?"

"Hey, please keep your voice down."

"Uncle Alex is not a factor. He doesn't even know."

"He must. He has the radar."

"Looks like you have it, Dad."

"Why would I? You have a girlfriend."

"We broke up. It ran its course."

"So you're free now. Heterosexuality ran its course."

"I like girls too. This is why they invented the word *bi*. And *queer*."

"You are losing me."

"Don't worry about me."

"I'm not worried. I'm processing the information. And I'm telling you. Keep it quiet. We're not in Canada. Got that?" Mirza nods, a sort of shrug-nod, not entirely acquiescent. Adem resumes eating, still indignant. "I'm not ignorant about this. I know it happens. Prison, the army. When there is no outlet. Guys need a release. They don't put a word on it. It doesn't always need a name or a parade every year."

"Dad ..."

"Bosnia is a different place."

"You think?"

His father points straight at him. "Just — be careful."

24

In a few days Mirza will drive to Tuzla with Damir. They've been hanging with each other more, and meanwhile less with the post-prayer gang. It's as if Damir is subbing for Kemo, for the Kemo that Mirza was hoping to find. Even his father seems glad not to see Kemo around much lately. They know he's been sparring with his sister Mirsada over her style of dress — the kind of joking that's really about coercion. Mirsada wears a head scarf only on the rare occasions she attends mosque. It seems clear that no man, least of all her little brother, will ever force her to hide her hair or face.

In Tuzla, Damir will settle some course-related stuff at the university, then the plan is to head east to Bratunac, where they will stay a night or two with Damir's aunts. Mirza's hope is to get them from there to Srebrenica, if Damir is willing. He has already arranged with his dad to use the Škoda. Adem is away all week with the truck, so he has no claim on the car. He has even given Mirza a little extra cash toward gas.

Over chats in the cafés, Mirza has been drawing Damir's story out. When the early months of the war became a living hell for Višegrad's Muslims, and Damir's father and brother were killed, his mother's family house outside Bratunac became their refuge. He and his mother and sister spent days and nights trudging through the forests and mountains east of Višegrad. The trails were filled with others fleeing the whole region. They got some handouts from UN troops but no offer of transportation. They passed through Srebrenica, its streets filled with refugees, and continued up the highway to his mother's people, who were among the lucky ones still in their own houses. Later they were forced from there too, and the whole family ended up in the Potočari camp on the edge of Srebrenica. The remaining men of the family died in the killings that July. Damir said the youngest was sixteen.

Mirza has told his own stories from the siege. Together they have found themselves recalling childhood events they shared but half forgot, things that happened in the neighbourhood after Damir's family moved in.

In the car on the highway to Tuzla they do not mention any of these things. They pass skeleton houses in abandoned villages. Mirza is surprised that after fifteen years many houses remain ruins. They only seem more stark by popping up among clusters of new, half-finished homes or tidy tracts of pristine stucco with real windows and paved driveways. Knowing the route well, Damir indicates now and then if a particular area is Muslim or otherwise. "Of course, I know also that Serbs were forced out of Sarajevo, and Krajina."

"Maybe the same Serbs are in these houses now."

Damir glances at him: "You're joking, yes?"

"Why would I joke? It's possible."

"Okay. Possible. But this part was overrun by Ratko Mladić's troops in the first month. Serbs living here never really experienced the war unless they put on a uniform, or helped the Chetniks kill their neighbours."

"Maybe they actually liked their Muslim neighbours."

"Did they save them?"

In a town nestled among rocky hills they stop at a *kafana* with outdoor tables. The espresso comes in demitasses embossed with a silhouette of a little Turkish boy. Mirza drank coffee from identical cups in Sarajevo and between planes in Vienna airport. He has no great love for double-boiled Bosnian coffee, and neither, it seems, do many Bosnians. Espresso is the default in the cafés if you don't specify. Damir always loads his with sugar, enough to make Mirza's teeth scream.

"Damir, what is this place?"

"Olovo."

"There's a Catholic church there, on the hill."

The red rooftops climb steeply toward two Romanesque spires with gold crosses. Nearby, a white minaret sticks up.

"There were Croats here. Probably they are gone now."

"I don't think I've ever been here."

"If you've been to Tuzla, you've come through Olovo — there's no other route."

"I've never been to Tuzla. We went the other way mostly, to the coast."

"Lucky guy. Mediterranean lifestyle!"

It's one in the afternoon, but no one on the small patio is eating lunch. Coffee is it. A table of three guys, older than Mirza and Damir, are surveying the street scene through their sunglasses. When one of them makes or answers a phone call, the other two wait a bit, then start playing with their own phones, which tends to make Damir do the same, then Mirza wants to reach for his, even though the last thing he needs is another text from his father. He scans the storefronts across the street, the stepped boxes of apples and plums and red peppers, the VWs and Mercedes and old Yugos and Zastavas at the curb. A Beemer SUV cruises by, tinted windows shut tight. The street is alive with shoppers and traffic but not in the busy way of Sarajevo. It's a

Thursday, but the pace feels like the weekend. Their own tiny patio is almost full. The sun filtering through the red umbrellas gives patrons a rosy tint.

"They sell Croatian beer."

"Hmm?" Damir's head comes up.

"Karlovačko." Mirza indicates the umbrella flaps, the brand displayed in medievalesque script. He may have been in Canada for twelve years, but he knows which beer is which.

One of the guys wearing sunglasses tilts his head at them: "Karlovačko." He raises an imaginary bottle.

On impulse Mirza raises his own toast: "Croatia!"

People turn their heads. The three dudes sit immobile in their impenetrable shades. One of them lifts his coffee cup and intones: "Bosnia." His friends, and Damir and Mirza, pick up their cups and solemnly echo the word.

He's still half-Canadian. He wishes it wasn't so obvious. But there seems to be a shrinking divide between before and after. His war dreams come more often now. And then there's what happens in his mind's eye, what's replayed by his other senses, when he is in certain places and he looks around and a memory surfaces.

Damir is driving now. Mirza is looking at the map, the same one he bought in Toronto. He has folded it into a neat tablet enclosed in a clear plastic zip-lock bag, showing their Sarajevo-to-Tuzla route on one side, Tuzla-Bratunac-Srebrenica on the other. His lips silently form the names of surrounding towns and villages: Požnarica, Križevići, Jelovo Brdo, Kruševo, Žaljenica, Simin Han. The rolled *r*'s, soft *š*'s, buzzing *ž*'s, the pleasure of making "Brdo" not come out "Bird-o." The almost ungraspable distinction between *ć* and *č*. In grade school they were drilled until the words lost meaning. *Ćevapčići i čaj*: kebabs and tea, kebabs and tea, kebabs and tea.

Jovan. The boy's name was Jovan. At the brewery. The one with the cart. This pops out of nowhere. Mirza stares at the map, as if there was a trigger in it. Why does he remember this now? Jovan had a long face and bad teeth and a black wisp of moustache. He seemed more like a peasant. Maybe he was a gypsy. Jovan was the meat and bone, the ropes of intestine, hanging in the gates of the brewery yard. Kemo said this later, many days afterward. It made sense. It explained why Jovan disappeared. He was out in the street with his cart, and then there was only the cart, unclaimed.

After the first shell and their frantic dash into a building across the street, Jovan went back outside to get the water jugs he'd just filled. Through the grimy cellar window they watched him. Then the street was a chaos of earth-shaking noise and flying debris. The window blew in. They lay on the dank floor of the storeroom with other people until it seemed that the two shells were all. It was usually one or two, the second one sent (or not) to punish the Samaritans helping the wounded. No third shell came. When they went out, there was a woman with only one leg being loaded into a car. Jovan's cart was there, and the mangled water jugs. In the bars of the gate, there was a mash of flesh, a body turned inside out. One of Jovan's blue and white Adidas was near the cart. The shoe didn't register as Jovan's until they talked about it later.

The hills and forests all around the highway are filled with villages. The war was out here too, but Mirza still knows almost nothing about that. The map shows a maze of back roads and paths between isolated hamlets. Every few kilometres there's a tiny white dot with a name. One is simply *Jabuka*: Apple. More than one place is named Waterfall. At *Klisura* (Gorge) a road dead-ends.

A part of Mirza wants to find these places, escape the highway and the shabby, characterless towns, the flashy new gas bars, the cookie-cutter raw brick and concrete houses. Are there still real peasants in Bosnia, people in pointy-roofed stone and timber houses without phones or cars or televisions? With sheep and goats for company? What is it like to live in a place accessed by footpaths? Were some of them remote enough to miss the war?

"We could go to Jabuka."

Damir glances at him.

"Honestly. It's a village, on the map."

"I think you will find nothing there. Not even apples."

"How do you know that?"

"My intelligent guess."

"In school they took us to a mountain village once. We had to hike from the bus."

"We went every summer with Uncle Avdo, to our cousins, up to Treskavica. I never went with school. My father's people came from those mountains, real ones, not like these hills. I heard someone is paying people now to live in the old stone huts. They rebuilt the destroyed ones. They pretend they are peasants."

"Fuck, no."

"They roast lambs for the tourists, sell them *kajmak* and *rakija*. They actually live in Goražde, when it's not the season."

"There must still be real peasants somewhere."

"Somewhere, but not there."

"You are one cynical guy."

"You think so? You are the one looking for mass graves."

"True. When we're in Bratunac, I want to go to the place where my uncle died. Žaljenica."

"I know it. There is an old mine there."

The university admin building in Tuzla brings to mind a sprawling 1960s high school in Toronto but with the unsettling addition of shrapnel scars. Damir parks in the drive looping into the main entrance.

"Do you want to come in? I will be an hour maybe."

"I'll wander."

Damir pulls out a key on a plastic fob: "For my room, if you get tired of wandering." He points out a low-rise residence building. "Room 203, second floor. You have to knock first, in case Omer is there."

Mirza does wander a bit on the school grounds, then to a large leafy park across the road. He follows a path toward buildings that turn out to be shops on a cobbled pedestrian street. The paving stones are new, the clean stucco facades painted pale yellow or tan. The side lanes, still scarred, seem stuck in mid-restoration.

Two Roma girls have set up in a square beside a dry fountain: one sings, the other sashays and whirls, stopping to tag after passersby for change. The song is a lament, something for a much older voice. The girl repeats the same few bars without variation, her voice shouting loud then slack as she loses breath. Mirza watches with a familiar gut feeling, his dismay at childhood misappropriated. The girls are in bright but grubby dresses, faces smudged, hair greasy. The mother is nearby, crouched by a grocery entrance with a baby in her arms.

People like to say the Gypsy fathers are at home drinking, watching soccer on their plasma TVs.

Mirza buys some juice and a bar of soap in the grocery. On the way out, he gives a coin to the woman with the baby. He finds a bench in the shade in the park and watches a faraway man cutting weeds with a scythe. He hasn't forgotten Damir's room number. He heads back and goes into the dorm building, climbs to the second floor, and knocks on the hollow door, the sound bouncing along the empty corridor. It's still August. He has seen only two others in the building, one an obvious caretaker. He lets himself in.

The scent is faintly locker room. The room is a symmetry, two beds made up with thin quilts, two small desks each with gooseneck lamp and bookshelf, two narrow doorless closets. The shelf on the right has a few textbooks on it: chemistry and mathematics. Through the window he can see the curving drive and his father's Škoda. He sits on the right-hand bed. On the wall above the opposite bed is a Dino Merlin concert poster. Mirza has never followed Bosnian pop stars, but he's heard of Merlin. He's known as a true *Bosanac*, Bosnia for all Bosnians.

He sits in the stuffy silence. Far off in the building someone is banging on the pipes. Under the window, between the beds, is a table unit with two drawers. The near drawer is slightly open, revealing the bright blue waistband of a pair of athletic shorts. Mirza almost reaches for them. He stands. He is leafing through a chemistry text when he feels the phone buzz against his thigh.

"Yeah."

"Hey, I'm free. Where are you?"

"In your room."

"Stay there."

"Sure."

"I'll come."

"Okay."

Mirza pockets his phone. He takes in a long breath and lets it out. He knows absolutely what is about to happen. He sits on the bed again. He's remembering. He stands and goes to the window. He can't see Damir crossing from the main building, but he is seeing him nonetheless: a new kid wandering into the wrecked apartment, and he and Kemo going at it on the foam pad, and the kid saying dumb kid things, throwing debris at them. The kid got sat on afterwards by Kemo and slapped a bit by Mirza until he cried for mercy and promised to keep his mouth shut, which as far as they know he did. A bit later, his family moved into the ruined flat.

Damir arrives. He drops his bag on the floor and plunks himself down on the bed. He leans back on his elbows, his head against the wall. They run through some meaningless talk about his courses. It's perfectly clear that Damir's cock has swelled to a hard ridge inside his jeans.

Mirza says, "Maybe I'll take a shower."

"There is no hot water."

"Bummer." Mirza says this in English, which makes them both laugh.

"Where is your roommate today?"

"With his parents. I called him."

"Is that far?"

"Extremely far."

25

In the morning they try to find the caretaker but end up showering quick and cold. Afterward, they go out to the park and find a bench in the sun. They just bask, almost mute. Eventually Damir stands up.

"We're going."

"What?"

"Coffee."

"Wait a bit."

"Up! Let's go!" Damir jogs in a little circle, then stops, standing between Mirza and the sun. His hair is a chestnut halo round his head.

Mirza says, "Only third time for me. With a guy."

"Oh? Really? I don't think so."

"No?"

"No. You live in gay marriage country."

"Exactly. No more hanky-panky."

"Translate."

"Now sex is only for the wife, or the husband. And for you?"

Damir laughs. "I am not married."

"I mean guys. How many?"

"I have never counted."

"So, if you don't mind, are you gay or ...?"

Damir looks around. A woman is staring in their direction while her dog pees. Damir sits on the bench again. "We should not say that word too much."

"Okay. Whatever. Let's get some breakfast."

That's it for the gay talk. Even in the privacy of the car, they leave it behind. Heading east out of Tuzla, Damir points out a spot where unarmed Serbian prisoners were massacred by Muslims.

"So you see, I'm not unfair to Serbs. Of course, Serbs got their revenge three years later, in the square."

Mirza remembers the Tuzla square bombing, probably the same square where he and Damir had their coffee and pastry. Most of the dead were teenagers. By then, late in the war, Mirza's mother had stopped trying to shield him from the TV images.

The day turns overcast, the air muggy under a grey blanket. Though they've again crossed the unmarked border into Republika Srpska, they still seem to pass as many reconstructed mosques as village churches. They come to a market sprawling in muddy

— *231* —

fields on either side of the highway. Cars are parked at careless angles on shoulders too narrow for it. The through traffic is slowed to a crawl. Adults and kids straggle back and forth across the road. A dog sitting on the pavement brings them to a halt, which decides for them that they will stop and take a break. A parking spot on the spongy grass costs one mark. The man advises them to take their bags from the back seat.

A barbeque stand is selling roasted corn. They buy two cobs from the vendor and wander past stalls of cheap clothing, kitchenware, toys, cleaning products, CDs, homemade brandy, trays of *burek* and barbecued meat, white rounds of cheese, baskets of red peppers and onions and muddy potatoes. It's half farm market, the other half basically the same stuff found in the dollar stores in Toronto. Mirza mentions this to Damir and gets a disbelieving look.

A sausage seller has some baked sheeps' heads on offer, one with its greasy paper wrapping opened to display the grinning skull and poached eyeballs. Hearing the accents, seeing the battered old Yugos and Fićas, Mirza knows he's among what city dwellers call *papci* — "hoofs." Sarajevans who refused to desert their hometown during the siege still grumble about the waves of backwoods refugees who settled in and lowered the city's cultural capital.

"Do you want to come to Žaljenica with me?"
Damir gives a sideways glance. "I could."

"We would have to go through Srebrenica."

"Yeah. I know your plan."

"Have you been recently?"

"We go to the burials in July. Potočari memorial."

"I saw it on TV. My uncle was killed near there, as a soldier. They never found him, but there is a stone for him."

"They have not found my cousins yet. We still go every year. I will go as long as my aunts are alive."

They pitch their chewed cobs with others in the weeds behind the stalls. It starts to spit rain. They head back to the car, which seems to be listing into the mud. The left front tire is flat. Mirza finds the spare. It's the inflated kind, which vaguely worries him. He wrestles with the jack and lug wrench while Damir stands over him. When he lowers the jack, the spare is half flat as well. They decide they can drive on it. A few people helpfully point out the obvious as they pull back onto the highway.

Underway, the Škoda seems desperate to veer into oncoming traffic. Mirza keeps his speed down, and cars pile up behind them. The curves and hills are no impediment to drivers who want to pass — more an incentive. An antique Audi labours past them and back into the lane just seconds from obliteration by a tanker truck. Three more cars pass them bumper-to-bumper. In his mirror Mirza watches others jockeying to be next out.

"Don't they care if they die horribly?"

"They don't think that far. It's like joining the army."

They exchange a glance, which makes Mirza drift left, then fishtail right again. The farmland recedes, and the road climbs into a winding course though rock cuts and forest. Mirza is worried about the tire. He pulls over, waits for the line of trucks and cars to whiz by, and gets out. The sidewall is burning hot to his touch.

"Shit."

Back in the driver's seat he consults the map, which shows a small town maybe ten kilometres away.

"You know anyone in this area?"

Damir shrugs. "In Zvornik. Not close."

They sit. The car gets steamy, and they crank open the windows. The drizzly air smells of diesel and damp forest.

Mirza says, "We should keep going."

"We could have some fun first."

Hearing this, Mirza is subtly shocked, but not unreceptive.

"You mean in the car?"

"No, out on the pavement. The centre line."

"But someone might stop. To assist us."

They look at each other and laugh. Mirza scans the road. There seems to be a turnoff up ahead to the right.

The rutted track leads up a gentle rise into the woods. When they crest the hill, they're looking down on a clearing packed with junked cars.

A very old, very thin man steps out of a shed and stares. He begins walking toward them: "*Nema! Nema Škode! Nema!*"

Mirza reverses the car, and they creep back over the hill.

In Vlasenica, they wait in a café while a garage fixes the flat.

Breaking a silence, Damir says, "You are not my first Canadian." He lets this hang in the air a moment. "A guy at the new multiplex, he was waiting there after the film. His name was John. We went to his hotel. He was a kind of NGO guy. In the war I heard there were some, you know, with the UN. Bosnian guys hooked up with them at Dobrinja Checkpoint, in exchange for cigarettes."

Mirza remembers: a pack of Marlboros meant food. The dilemma was whether to smoke, or barter them to get meat or coffee.

26

There is one traffic light in Bratunac. Damir calls it by the Bosnian *semafor*, even when speaking English. They drive through it several times over their two-day stay, and Damir refers to it with mock reverence: "The *Semafor* of Bratunac." His two aunts, widowed sisters, share a three-room house set back from the main road leading south to Srebrenica. They look to Mirza like old peasant women with their head scarves and baggy clothes and knotted faces.

The aunts have much to ask about Damir's mother and his studies in Tuzla and his summer in Sarajevo. Mirza tunes out their chatter and sips the boiled coffee and the little glasses of fluorescent-orange juice, the same brand his mother bought twenty years ago. They keep encouraging him to sugar his coffee, as if he doesn't quite grasp the concept.

For dinner they have a fresh-killed chicken from neighbours down the road, home-baked bread, and mounds of kale fried up with onion and garlic. The neighbour couple, Serbs, drop by with brandy after the meal and hear Mirza's story of coming back to work for his father and his plan to visit Žaljenica and the Srebrenica memorial at Potočari.

The two visitors have barely exited the house when Aunt Amela says, "Those two were no help in the war. Now they give us eggs."

"And firewood," adds Damir.

"A little, yes."

The aunts don't drive, so next morning they all go out to do some stocking up at a farm market and the Konzum in Zvornik. Though it's a Friday, there seems to be no plan to attend mosque.

Mirza mentions it to Damir. Is it because they have houseguests?

"They don't always go to mosque. They will observe Ramadan, of course."

Late in the afternoon they pack food and juice and drive ten minutes to a picnic area, a broad pebbly beach on a curve of the Drina. It's a perfect August evening, the air still, late sunlight slanting through the trees. There are some boys horsing around on a rocky outcrop by the river, finding big stones and heaving them into the water. The names they shout to each other are Serbian.

Mirza has not and will not ask the aunts exactly what happened to them at the hands of Serbs. It's simple enough: they lived in terror for a few years, and then Ratko Mladić came in and killed their men over the age of fifteen. Mirza also knows that the Muslim-occupied parts of this region were ruled by a thug named Orić, who burned Serb villages and killed their inhabitants. In Sarajevo, Alija Izetbegović called Orić away from his post just days before Mladić moved in and murdered thousands. Some say that Srebrenica and its Muslims were bartered away to the Serbs by Izetbegović in exchange for Serb-held suburbs of Sarajevo, that Alija, being devout, knew that the martyred Muslims would be rewarded in Heaven. Now Izetbegović is dead, Mladić is still at large after thirteen years, and Radovan Karadzić is telling lies to the Hague Tribunal.

Mirza's vague ruminations on these matters fade as he watches the hooting boys on the rock. Their limbs are lit golden by the evening sun. In a year or two, their voices will be changing. Right now, there is no other thought in their minds but how big a rock they can carry, how big a splash it will make. They would have been babies during the war, or not even. Without warning Mirza is hit with emotion: envy and longing, like a body blow. The war stole this from him. Along with everything else, it stole the last of his boyhood summers.

Now Damir is passing him a paper plate with hunks of dense bread and sliced sausage and a big creamy dollop of *kajmak*.

"What is your job in Toronto, Mirza?" Aunt Hana pours him some juice.

"I'm an artist." Mirza says this with practised confidence, making it matter.

Hana nods, her eyes shifting away.

Damir says, "He's doing a thing about Srebrenica."

"Partly. Really it's just about war."

"And politics."

"Politics, yes. It's complicated." Should he elaborate? He wants them to know there is nothing bogus about him. The aunts busy themselves with the food, their eyes lowered to the tasks. "The UN is to blame, naturally, and foreign leaders, and Bosnia's leaders. Military leaders too, of course ..." The silence stretches, until Mirza says, "Could Izetbegović have saved Srebrenica?" He hears his words like they come from somewhere else, from an outsider. But he's not that. He is a Sarajevan.

Amela's jaw clenches. "No one saved us. We were lambs to the slaughter. We were nothings. Clinton came here to Potočari and made a speech. He looked sad for us, and then he went away, and again we were nothings, our men were still in the ground. Those boys over there, they will be the new Chetniks. I hope I will be gone by then."

At the cemetery in Potočari, Mirza is at a loss for how to respond. There are thousands of identical marble stones, brilliant white with pyramidal tops, in perfect rows. They converge to a vanishing point against orchards and blue sky and green hills. It's like a gigantic sculptural work demonstrating the mystery of perspective. It's actually beautiful, laying out its symmetry before him in the clear sunlight. He seems unable to absorb what it actually signifies. He brings his gaze back from the distant points of white vanishing into summer green, all the way back to the pillars not twenty feet from him, with impeccably rendered names and dates.

He was expecting some mourners or maybe a few foreign tourists, but the only life present is three workers in overalls among the newest graves, replacing wooden markers with the freshly carved stones. In a way, he is glad he's alone here. The aunts have some visiting to do in Srebrenica, so Damir went with them in the car and left him here at the cemetery with a promise to fetch him in an hour or so. Then they will drive the few kilometres to Žaljenica.

He stands now at the memorial wall, following with his eyes its massive half-circle of sloping grey granite, carved with 8,372 names of the dead and still missing. The number is disputed. Some claim it's too high by hundreds or thousands, that many were ordinary combat deaths. He knows too that there are Serb graveyards nearby full of unsung victims, though in far lesser numbers.

The first carved name is Abdurahmanović. There are seven of those. Next come four for Abidović.

Then almost two columns for Ademović. He counts: the name is carved ninety-eight times. Mirza knows that Osmanović, his family name, is fairly common. Proceeding to the *O*'s, he finds sixteen Osmanovićs. Is he related to some of them? No one has said so. But there is a lot that hasn't been said.

He goes back to wander through the gravestones. In his mind he puts it into words. "These are lives. Each stone is a life." He's thinking it is fitting that the stones are so luminous, that people can come here and weep and in the same moment be in a place that gathers and concentrates light.

As he walks back to the entry gates, a minibus pulls into the lot and a dozen or so passengers emerge, all women except for the driver and two boys of maybe ten and twelve, who have the look of being pulled away from things that boys would rather do. The woman are young to very old, some in the traditional peasant garb and head scarves of Damir's aunts.

There is no stone with Uncle Medo's name at Žaljenica, or none that they can find. They find only an abandoned mine entrance plugged with boulders, some ruined buildings and the foundations of houses, and an old man picking weeds. He tells them that the plants are for medicinal tea. They ask about the memorial stone, but he can't help them.

Heading back to the house, Damir at the wheel, Mirza takes out a bottle of plum brandy he got at the market, a plastic pop bottle still with its Coke screw cap. He opens it and takes a hit, tucking his chin to force the swallow. He offers the bottle to Damir: "Looks like water, burns like fire."

Damir shakes his head.

"Hey, why not? Are you Bosnian or what?"

"That is an insult to the honour of Bosnian drivers."

"What insult? They drive like they're drunk anyway."

Damir smiles slightly at this. "Fuck you."

Mirza takes one more swig and stashes the bottle away. This way of drinking — the rotgut brandy, the car, the incitement to a driving friend — it's unlike him. It undoubtedly has to do with this trip, the place, the cemetery, whatever is bouncing around inside him, but the core of it seems now almost to be exhilaration.

He turns and looks at Damir, and this very act, just observing his friend's pensive face, hair whipping in the warm wind, eyes glancing at him with assessment, irony, judgement — this seeing of Damir at this moment in the sun-filled car with the meadows and trees whizzing past — holds everything that has happened to them and between them since the day they first said hello at Željo's. Damir is the Kemo that was supposed to be. Mirza has even called him Kemo by mistake — which made him scowl.

The aunts are staying in Srebrenica. Ramadan begins soon, and they will kick it off with the other women of *Srebreničke Majke*. They will find their own way home, and Mirza and Damir will return to Sarajevo. Mirza will go back to work for his father, and in less than two weeks, Damir will head back to Tuzla to begin classes. Since their overnighter in Damir's room they have been doing an odd dance around the sex issue. The presence of Damir's aunts, of course, has been a damper, but in any case, Mirza is not making moves. From the start, the cues have come from Damir. It's seems maybe they will be just friends, for now. Mirza does not want to force anything.

PART FOUR

27

Here is some food. Pero looks at the plate of cheese and pickles and a bread roll. His son is pacing, talking on the phone. And the woman too (his daughter?) in the front hall, talking. There are two phones, and they are both talking at once. Mirza this, Mirza that. Everything is about Mirza. The voices are strained. The hard cheese is the wrong colour. The pickles are too sweet. But it's food.

There are photographs in a large book on the table. The place is called Makarska, and the word is right there over the pictures. He knows the place somehow. He knows the photos. He feels good when he looks at them. It's like getting under a familiar old blanket. Strange that he knows this place but only in pictures. On the other hand, the place he is in right now, with this cheese and bread and the telephoning and the upset, he can't seem to get used to it. He knows it, but he can't remember it. Here it is. That's all.

His son is off the telephone now.

I find my sister still standing over the phone in the hall.

"Krista, what exactly did you send to him?"

"I can't talk about it."

"Do you want to tell me what happened?"

"Talk more to Adem if you want. Phone him back."

Kristina goes out the front door and into the beautiful late-summer morning. A moment later she's back.

"Don't phone him. I'll send you the whole thing. As soon as I'm home. I'm sorry."

"You don't need to be sorry —"

She's gone, leaving the door ajar.

I do some tidying in the kitchen. I go outside and water the window boxes, check the back gate. I come in and get my father some ice cream, then leave him and go up to my study. I spend some time browsing news sites and, for a ludicrous few minutes, porn. When I check my inbox, there are two forwards from Krista.

Adem,

I want you to reassure me that Mirza cannot access your mail. Please change your password if you have to. I'm sending you something after you reply to this.

Krista

Dear Adem,

Thanks for replying.

I'm going to try not to filter this because that has been the problem all along. There are things I shared with the group at COSTI. I mean the rape group. It's hard to write that word, hard to think it, and I know it's hard for you to hear it again. I'm finally raising this because it helps explain why I have been the way I've been. Not just me. It explains what we have been, you and me and Mirza, since the thing we call the war, everything that happened in those four years. It explains why Mirza is there now even if he doesn't know what happened or exactly why he is going back. We have pretended to let go of all that. You know more about what happened to me in that one week than I know about your entire time, years, out there with the army. But you still know only a little. We know only scraps of each other.

I can see you right now in my mind. You are staring at these words like they've already done you an injustice. The unsaid things have been there through all our dinner silences and dinner chatter and whatever good times we've welcomed — the need to leave it all behind and hope that Mirza would too. I don't know how we thought that was possible. Especially with Daddy there always. He was the obvious wound, always present. Whatever was in Mirza's head all those years, we made almost no effort to access it.

And of course, the unspoken is entirely related to what "our" army was fighting for, the mess of Izetbegović's failures and the little jihad he smuggled into our country. You said, eventually, that you thought Alija was almost as bad for Bosnia as Karadžić. You said, after Grbavica, that maybe we could try to leave. Then the subject was dropped, and I didn't push it. You could not desert your army comrades and who was I to argue? Now, Mirza suddenly wants to sort all of this out. You've seen pictures of his installation piece. He is obsessing about the killings and "genocide" and exhumations, and ultimately I blame us for this. Whatever we decided, it has always been our habit to evade the issues each time Mirza starts talking about it. He was a child. Now he's with you in that place of grief and evil (I can't see it any other way regardless of what has changed), and maybe you are sharing old stuff — I mean new stuff, things that have never yet been held up to view. At COSTI, I did hold them up to view. If I talked about it when I came home, you changed the subject.

Mirza wanted me to open up, especially in these recent months. My inability to talk with him about it (my horrible, shameful secret) has helped push him away. Please take care of him, Adem. He's still like a child inside. We know his friend Kemo is a Serb-hater and an Islamist. I don't know if you looked at the latest stuff I sent you, the links that Mirza gets from Kemo. "The fatherland of a Muslim is wherever Sharia prevails." It's essentially variations on that plus revenge fantasies. Kemo has become like his brother and father. He is avenging their deaths. He and his mother probably think still, because of the ridiculous lies, that I was a spy for the Serbs — a mole for my hero Karadžić! It's so stupid, a fatal stupidity. I saw through Kemo's polite cold facade with me two summers ago here in our own house. If Mirza and he are still in touch, you might want to have a talk about it, some casual questions maybe. He will not listen to me.

I'm finished with blaming myself. Years of irrational blame that I was stupid to go out to help an old friend, that I was careless enough to be caught and then tortured by animals who thought they were men. I told the COSTI women the same things that I heard back from them. There were women from Rwanda across the hall. We felt almost lucky by comparison. But all of it was completely outside the paltry fact of whose women we were, Serbs or Muslims or anything else. The kinds of things, the physical things that these animals thought up, to do to a woman, they can't be spoken about to men who actually love women. I will never be able to say to you what happened to us, Adem. Now you have found someone over there who maybe is less damaged. I don't know. We don't know each other now. We know what we were, to some degree.

Adem, believe me, I know you have not escaped this. You experienced things you will never speak of. You know I know, but I have to say it, so you can see I don't disregard your suffering to focus on my own. There are ways of not thinking about it, but I can't seem to get away from the relapses. I have been told recently that I may have clinical depression. The doctor says (what I already know) that it's difficult to separate true mental illness from disorder in people who have had war or rape trauma or whatever kinds of horrors that trigger normal responses. You have channelled or diverted your normal responses into meting out justice and re-entering the Bosnian business world (my neutral description). I have hardly a clue of what you did "out there" in the war, either the fighting or the dealing. Or why your old friend/associate, the murderer, raper, rapist, decided to get back at you through me. He gave me especially degrading treatment because I was your wife. They knew better than to scar me physically to the extent of the other women.

I'm glad you had a hand in Ćelo's death. I know you did it for me and for many others too. Ćelo was a true believer in rapism. I saw it for seven days up close. It has nothing to do with nationalism or Islamism or the outcome of a war. He didn't even pretend to be a proper Muslim.

It's only about revenge and infinite power. Physical power over women and revenge against their men. It's part of an ideology that says men and women occupy completely opposed belief systems and that women and their system are worth less than shit. They told us we were exactly that, and they had shit available for the comparison. A big joke. And people point out that Muslim and Croat women suffered the same from Serb goons. Yes. Yes. Even more, far more. But this point doesn't help anyone. The problem is men.

The outline of what happened to us, to the women in the motel, is in the COSTI documentation, attached. You don't need to open it, but it's there. You are my son's father, and we are the ones who protected him and got him through the war alive. We loved each other. We still need to watch out for him. I don't know what Mirza knows, what he might have asked you there or what you have told him. I can't imagine what it's like for the two of you to be back in the apartment. Is it the same? Did your cousins take care of it? I really don't know what to think about it except that whatever Mirza gets from this, what he hears from other people, bitter people, it will only take him deeper into everything we tried to escape. I know Ćelo's people are still there, or others like them, in black-market and in the Federation government too. The money guys. And then all the little Chetniks too, the Ratko-lovers, and the new Saudi-style Islamists. The generation that we wanted Mirza never to become a part of. The whole quagmire that you have chosen to return to and now invited your son to as well. Maybe he is meeting some good people. You would know that. I hope you would know.

Of course you feel put-upon by this, betrayed even — I mean *prevario* more than *izdao* because you have a deal-maker's understanding of emotions. Profit and loss. You've heard this from me before. You've never taken it to heart. But I know you won't let Mirza get into trouble. Please pay attention to him, what he's up to. I have no confidence that you are planning to return here in the near future, and as long as Mirza is there, you certainly need to be there too. I'm sure you are getting by there, just as you were here. Should we stop this pretence that you and I are still mutually supporting? Alex has helped with a lump payment toward the mortgage. He did well from Lyle's estate, better than you might think. If you remember, he forgave us the remaining debt for the down payment. Alex, bless him, is helping to keep me sane.

You don't need to open the attachment. I don't think it will fix anything. It's your decision. I think that you already know all this about Ćelo. You only don't know about my week with him, them. If anyone deserves to die, it is these men. You doled out justice, did your part at last, and now I do understand why you would want to push the thoughts away. I'm also to blame for never telling you the full story, but that was not possible for me.

Next April in Makarska, we have a chance to be a family again for a few weeks. I hope you will arrange your schedule to make sure you're around. Not in and out, but really there. This is not an accusation, only a reminder and a request.

I used English here because it's still my first language, and I wanted things to be very clear. That's all. It's not meant as any sort of statement. I really don't know if I'm English or Bosnian or Canadian. I feel like a kind of nothing right now. Definitely, I feel like your former wife, and I don't

think that will surprise you. You are a
Bosnian. I want no part of that world
anymore. We never really bridged the gap.
Makarska is different. It's a special place,
and I want to see my family together there
at least one more time.

Krista

I open Kristina's attachment. It describes a "rape
centre" near Sarajevo run by paramilitaries. There
are interviews with eight women identified by
initials. Some of them, including "K.O.," mention
a boss man who came and went and who the other
men called Ramo or Ćelo. I start reading the
interview with "K.O." She describes coming from
Grbavica and being taken off the street by armed
men and held in a room, questioned about her activities, her husband, her UN pass, then she is put
into the back of a truck with some other women.
They tie her wrists behind her back before putting
her in the truck. This image stalls me. I see it
clearly, as if I'm there beside the truck or watching
a film I've seen about the war or another war.
These films are about my sister. I can't and won't
read any more of this. I close the attachment. I copy
the text of Krista's message to a new email and
send it to myself. I permanently delete the message
with the attachment.

My sister. This happened to her. She said "clinical depression." She said "that place of grief and evil." The place where her husband and son are now, without her.

I can hear my father downstairs, moving around in the kitchen, cursing about something, though not yet with the urgency that will draw me downstairs to check on him. Lyle is here too, looking at me from his framed photo on the bookshelf. He seems like a dream I once had.

28

The restaurant is at Yonge and St. Clair, a place Lyle and I used to like in the first decade of our life in Canada. It has moved a few doors away from where it was in the 1980s, and I'm glad of this. I can avoid specific associations while still paying some homage to that time and to the old neighbourhood.

It's been years since I sat with my sister in a restaurant, just her and me. Having her to the house today seemed too risky, or too private. I don't want to know more about what happened. I only want to glean what state she's in.

I've booked a corner banquette. The venue is ideal, an experience in civilized dining that faces extinction in a city filled with people shouting through blasting music over cold hard little tables in rooms with the aesthetic appeal of shipping containers.

We have ordered and received our wine. The bottle is in a chilled Thermos bucket. Just its presence makes me feel hopeful. I raise a glass.

"To my brave sister."

"Or crazy."

"Not at all. Too sane. You've been incredibly forthright. I have to tell you that I didn't read the attachment. The letter was enough." At this my eyes unexpectedly tear up.

Krista regards me warily. "I'll be all right. Please don't worry. I feel like a weight is off, just opening up about it."

As I swallow my emotion, Krista rolls a hit of Chardonnay around in her mouth: "Is this Australian?"

"New Zealand."

"It's good. Did you know that Mirza is gay?"

This actually makes my wine go down the wrong way.

"Did I know? I certainly did not know. How do you know?"

"He told his father in Sarajevo."

"I'm surprised. You may not think so, but ... In fact, we did have a drink once on Church Street."

"Why was that?"

"He wanted to talk about moving out, about your plan to sell."

"I've changed my mind."

"Have you? I don't think he has."

"That's pretty clear."

I toss off, "Well, that makes two in the family. Not so uncommon."

She nods vaguely.

"If he were here, we could celebrate."

Krista looks at me: "If he were here, it might be *worth* celebrating."

"It can't have been easy telling Adem."

"He never let on to you?"

"Not a word. It did cross my mind."

"Actually, he told Adem he's bisexual."

"That may be a strategy."

"Well, the present issue is his location." She picks up her wine and puts away a substantial gulp, places the glass neatly back in its circular dent in the tablecloth. I see the alcohol's gentle hit in her eyes as she looks around the restaurant: "We came here once. Years ago. For a birthday."

"Yours. I used to come here with Lyle. Way back. It was around the corner then."

"I was thinking about you and Lyle. How I could have married an Englishman. Do you remember Edward?"

"From Tooting. The astronomer."

"No. That was Nigel."

"Oh dear, yes. Nigel. He was a classic weed. Prematurely in tweed." This gets a small smile from Krista. "Was he marriageable?"

"No. But sweet. He talked about the moons. All the moons. Dozens of them."

"You could have had little Nigels, instead of Mirza."

"Unthinkable."

"Lyle was a bit more toff than tweed."

"Can't you be both?" Krista angles her head at a memory. "I think I only saw you once with Lyle, the Olympics visit."

"Twice. Makarska. Your wedding."

"Sorry. Of course."

"It was Lyle's fault, really. I mean, not being seen more. He had no interest in Yugoslavia."

"Why would he?"

"I hardly had. Only after you went back."

"You should have come more to Makarska, in the summers."

"Should've, yes."

Krista drifts into thought. "I can remember loving Adem." Her face is neutral, as if emotion is drained from the subject. "I was swept away. He used to be so thoughtful. Attentive. It was like a long holiday, not just the summers. In Sarajevo too. The Olympics ... Mirza ... But I was — really, I was essentially a trophy to him. Trophy and cook. He's a Balkan male. That's his essence."

"Meaning?"

"Among other things, the girlfriends."

"You don't have to be Balkan for that."

"No." Krista pauses, slowly rotating her wine-glass. "In fact, the war brought us closer again, at first."

"You looked out for each other."

She gives me a flat look, then disappears into

her thoughts. Eventually, she says, "I get, some days, kind of sucked under. I mean, much worse lately. I'm considering a therapist. I went back to COSTI, just to see what's available."

"Good," I say lamely. "I'm glad."

The food comes. Our chat moves to lighter things. She works on her grilled salmon while I hoover up my pasta and steal her potatoes.

Krista says, "How's Daddy?"

"Fine. The same."

"I hope he's not driving you crazy."

"He is. But those old holiday photos are a good focus. He seems to know that we're going there, that it's part of his world, past or present or whatever. But he still drives me crazy."

"Better you than me."

"Actually, I agree."

Out on the sidewalk it's a lovely September day, all back-to-school brisk and sunny. We stand adjusting to the light and traffic. Neither of us has anywhere we need to be. Maybe something more could happen. A movie? Instead, I say, "You know, Lyle is just up the street."

"I didn't know. Or maybe I forgot."

"I wouldn't mind dropping in on him. I won't cry. It's just a nice place to visit, to take a walk. Some lovely flora."

Krista gives me a sidelong glance. Her face is a flash out of childhood. "No fauna?"

"Squirrels. Birds."

"Are birds fauna?"

"Not sure. We'll ask."

"*Mount Pleasant.*"

"Doesn't it sound lovely?"

"But where's the Mount? All right, let's go see the squirrels. I mean Lyle."

"Squirrels dug up his bulbs. He called them tree rats."

29

I have never (almost never) doubted that Mirza was as straight as his own father. We were all thrown off, of course, by the girlfriend. But I can say that the few times I saw them together I sometimes found Jen a little testy with Mirza, and him giving it back. Maybe the truth about Mirza was in the air, well before I knew. I don't think anyone blames the gay uncle. Maybe Adem, a little, but he knows it can't be mentioned. In any case, I've been single for thirteen years and all but celibate for long stretches — not quite a reasonable role model for a carnally possessed teen. I have sought sex now and then since Lyle, but never love. I hardly need say that my nephew and I never discussed these matters.

Mirza came in one night — he was about sixteen or seventeen — when I was with an occasional hook-up, Roger. Mirza always had a key and knew he had a place to crash, but on this particular night, we were in the guest bedroom because the TV was there and Roger wanted porn. When I came down in the morning, Mirza was at the kitchen table.

He'd slept on the living room sofa. I could only think of him lying there hearing the grunts and moans and ridiculous dirty talk of the porn tape drifting down the stairs, and then Roger passing by the living room on his way out. I probably blushed for the first time in years. I said something like, "Now you know my secrets." Mirza just did a show of hey, cool, whatever, and focussed on his cereal.

A few summers ago I threw a family get-together in the back garden, a barbeque. It happened to be July, the tenth anniversary of Srebrenica, but the meal wasn't meant to honour anything, certainly not the massacre or Adem's brother, who'd been part of the effort to stop it. But the Srebrenica memorial events and old video clips were in the news, and I'm sure we didn't get through the meal without some reference to them. We finished eating, and I was encouraged to relax while others did the clearing and washing up. ("Others" meaning Krista and Mirza: my father and Adem would of course be out on the front porch, where Adem went to smoke.)

So I found myself alone, a bit drunk, staring at the flowers in the evening light, with Lyle's absence/presence moving through me the way it did every July, mixed to some degree, as every July, with the humbling vastness of Bosnia's grief, my family's grief. Back in 1995, with all of them stranded in Sarajevo, Lyle and I had watched the terrible Srebrenica reports together. A week or so later he was dead. Now, it all came back again, despite my half-conscious attempt to displace the memories with a jolly family party.

Mirza came out into the yard. I glanced at him and he stopped. He pretended he hadn't seen me wiping my face, and I pretended I hadn't seen him seeing it. I waited for him to go back into the house, and he did. A bit later Krista was sitting beside me.

"Are you all right?"

I might have been fine if she hadn't asked.

"Lyle," I said. "Lyle." I was addressing him, out there with the roses.

"Yes."

Suppressing the ridiculous sounds my throat wanted to make, I waved my arm at the garden: "This ..."

"Yes."

"All this ..."

"I know."

Krista put her hand on my arm. We sat quietly and I regained control.

"I'm such a baby. What do I have to cry about now?"

"Okay, it's okay." She sounded tired. "Do you want some pie?"

I told Krista I wanted pie.

Mirza brought my pie out, along with his own piece. Krista had whipped up some cream, and I could smell the brandy in it. We tucked in.

"It's the best, Uncle. You always make the best strawberry rhubarb pie."

"Easy on the rhubarb is the trick."

"And only the red stalks."

"You remember."

When the family lived with me in '96, Mirza sometimes watched while I baked. Now, through a mouthful of pastry he said, "I remember Lyle."

"You mean from Sarajevo?"

"Makarska."

"He was never there, Mirza, except for your parents' wedding."

"He had tinted glasses. Like Bono."

"Yes, he did, for a while."

"He talked about being on a boat. It was some kind of doctors thing."

Of course. Lyle had gone to a conference, in Venice. They took a boat tour down the Dalmatian coast. He was so close he couldn't *not* visit the in-laws.

"I'd completely forgotten."

"It was quick, maybe a day or two. We took him to see the Glamoč monument."

"I hope he was properly impressed."

Krista came out with Pero. She sat him across from us with a plate of pie and a shot glass of brandy. My father glanced at me and Mirza as he ate, as if he wasn't sure we were trustworthy.

Mirza said, "Do you think you would have married Lyle? If you could've?"

"I don't know. Might have. It wouldn't have changed anything."

Mirza nodded and, thank God, knew well enough to leave the subject.

30

Mirza's father heaves a sack of cement into the truck bed. "Finish with these, will you? I need to make a call."

Mirza should have got in ahead of him with the first sack, but a few seconds of hesitation landed them in the familiar pattern: how to keep Adem's bad back out of trouble while never referring to it. Mirza finishes the loading, half-listening to his father on the phone: something about the Dobrun site. Adem ducks into the supply shed, lowering his voice a few notches. When he comes out, he's ending the call.

"Why didn't you wait for Ljubo at the site last time?"

"I waited. I had to leave."

"He's got a job for you. You can talk about it today."

"Today?"

"That's where the load is going."

"Will he be there?"

"If he's not there, you'll wait. He's going to set you up supervising some guys at the yard in Brodar.

You'll be like a dispatcher. Just in the mornings."

This is not encouraging news to Mirza. It will only get him deeper into the "industry," as his father keeps calling it.

In Dobrun, the site is unchanged except for a fresh pile of bricks, of a different type, stacked on the concrete pad. The bricks Mirza brought weeks ago seem to be missing. He finds a spot where he can back up the pickup, more or less level with the platform. He drags the bags of cement out of the truck bed. He has been told that Ljubo will call.

An hour or so passes. Mirza briefly plays around with his phone's pathetic Web browser. He stares at some sheep grazing across the road. He phones and texts Damir, to no response. Finally a car pulls in. It's Vuk and a female friend.

"Hey, Miki, you are here!"

"I am. I'm guarding the bricks."

"Ljubo is coming. He told me to tell you. I can't stay. Taking my sister to Rogatica."

The girl smiles thinly.

Mirza says, "Would you happen to be working at Brodar these days?"

"Sometimes, yeah. How did you know?"

"Ljubo wants me to work for him. Dispatcher."

"Huh? I don't know. He will tell you."

"Do you happen to have his number?"

"He will call. See you! Maybe at Brodar!"

The dusty car bumps back onto the road, and Mirza is left alone with the sheep. A bit later he does get a call from Ljubo, who instructs him to drive to the same *bife* where the policeman bought him lunch on his last trip. He's rattling along the road toward the highway when another call comes, from his father.

"Did you see Ljubomir?"

"I'm meeting him. Five minutes."

"Don't go. Forget it. Just come home."

"He's waiting for me at his café."

"I'll deal with it. Did you leave the cement already?"

Mirza knows what's coming. "Yes."

"Bring it back."

When Mirza wheels into the supply yard, he can see his father moving around inside the cramped office by the gates. He joins his dad, and they head across the road to a gas bar with a café attached. Adem does meaningless shoptalk until they're seated with their coffee.

"Everything's off with Ljubo, the whole arrangement. You'll just work for me."

"Can you maybe pay me a little more?"

"I could pay you more if there were no fucking Ljubos in the world."

"What happened?"

Adem stares at him. "You are going to hear something someday, or maybe you already did. About your mother and the motel. Do you know what I'm talking about?"

"No."

"It was not only Ćelo. There was a place, they called it Blue Lagoon."

Mirza has read about Blue Lagoon on the Web. Women were enslaved. "She was there?"

"A week. She was just a day or two in Grbavica. When she came out, Ćelo took her off the street. Ljubo helped to close the place down later. He told me, and I checked it out, and it's true. Him and maybe twenty other guys. He thinks I owe him favours now because he's a hero. But fuck him. He was there for the raid on the motel, that's all. He was still a fucking Chetnik whatever else he did." Adem lights a cigarette and sucks in the smoke like a hit of oxygen. "She sent me something. Documents from COSTI. About the motel and what happened. But I have always known about it. It's not a thing we could ever discuss. She still blames me because I had dealings with Ćelo. I want you to know, Mirza, I do not blame myself. The rapists are to blame. The war is to blame. I am not to blame."

Mirza is staring at the tabletop now. He can listen, but it seems he cannot speak, cannot even look at his father.

Adem lays some cash on the table. "Did you get lunch? Have something. Have a beer. You can take the car. I have business with Hus." He stands. "You can forget work for a few days, okay?"

"Sure."

"Mirza, look at me."

Mirza looks up. There's nothing in him, nothing but numbness, no anger or tears or anything so helpful.

His father says, "I'm sorry you had to know this."

"Yeah. I'm sorry too."

"Understood. But you cannot be more sorry than I am. Believe me, I'm sorry that I cannot stop this shit, stop a war, that I cannot perform miracles."

People in the café are looking at them.

"It's okay, Dad. I don't blame you."

His father's face seems not to respond to this. He just glances sharply around the café, making people return to their business.

After Adem goes, Mirza simply feels blank. He stares out at the parked cars, the Dobrinja apartment towers, a plane rising from Butmir. The scene could be suburban Toronto. He sees his father's figure standing at the roadside. Adem jogs out and stops on the centre line, traffic boxing him in, until someone slows for him and he crosses to safety.

31

FIS Kultura is near the river on a short street lined with old Austro-Hungarian office blocks. A few steps lead Mirza and Damir down to an entrance manned by a hefty guy with a headset. They are supposed to show ID to prove that Damir is on the email invite list, but the muscle guy is chatting with two gothish women and just waves them past. Heat and smoke and noise blast up the curving stairway as they descend. The small room at the bottom is already crammed with bodies. The invite has billed it as a "gay/str8 disco party" with a 1980s theme. Damir says they happen three or four times a year, the location chosen for its distance from other bars and clubs.

Damir leads Mirza through the crowd to a bar alcove tended by a lithe young guy and an older woman. When they have their beer, they find a spot by the wall near the bar and stand surveying the crowd. Damir glances at Mirza with a look that says, *Pretty wild, huh?* He shouts into Mirza's ear, "See anyone you know?"

Mirza can only laugh. Who does he really know in Sarajevo except Damir and Kemo? If any childhood schoolmates were here, would he even recognize them?

"Maybe I should get out more."

"You will. I can't come every weekend from Tuzla. Unfortunately."

They drink and watch. There are as many women as men in the crowd. The dance area fills most of the room, gyrating kids sharing the floor with some old enough to be their parents.

Damir leans in and says, "I'm taking a look around," and he's gone in the crush.

Mirza lets the music pulse through him. In his nearly two months here he might have made more friends if he'd found Kemo's circle more congenial — or if he'd spent fewer evenings online grazing war sites and porn. Damir has actually helped pull him out of a slump. He realizes that he's been thinking of this night as a kind of date, a progression in the friendship. But Damir now seems more interested in circulating.

Mirza chugs the rest of his beer and joins the dancers. The music is short on Balkan flavours — the point, of course, is to take the crowd somewhere else. A guy comes up beside him, bopping his head to the music. His shaved skull is glistening with sweat, his sheer T-shirt stretched over pumped-up shoulders and pecs. He could easily have stepped right off Church

Street in Toronto. A moment's eye contact tells Mirza he's being cruised. He's not sure he's interested. He'd rather have the kid behind the bar with the sloppy shirt and bed-head. The man eventually moves away. Mirza digs out his phone and finds a text: *I'm on the terrace.*

He gets two beers, one for Damir. The bar boy points out a corridor leading to some stairs. He ends up in a gravelled courtyard with tables and scattered partiers. Beyond a high wall he can hear a tram rattling past on Kulina Bana. Even this open space is secluded from the public eye. He spots Damir with a woman and joins them.

"Mirza, Lola."

"Hey, Mirza." Lola looks him over. "You're double drinking."

"You want one?"

"I have Viljamovka." She raises a brandy glass.

"Then the beer is yours, Damir."

Mirza sits and they all clink glasses.

"Lola works for Gap. They have a store in the new mall, by the cinema."

"Come on Saturday," says Lola. "Opening sale." She takes out a Camel and tilts the pack to Mirza.

"Thanks, but I quit. I know that's un-Bosnian of me."

"Pah, you are smart."

"So I'm just curious. Is this actually a gay bar?"

Lola says, deadpan, "There are no gay bars in Sarajevo."

"Not Ribica?"

"Nooooo." She laughs.

Damir looks at Mirza: "You've been to Ribica?"

"With Kemo. It was the first place he took me."

"Because it's cool. But I'm surprised. He doesn't go there."

Lola says, "I know why you think it's gay, but no."

"Two hipster kind of guys were eyeballing me."

Lola says, "So they could be gay, but Ribica is not gay. Artistic, yes. They are hip and artistic like a hemorrhage. I've been there. I took my boss there. But they kick out guys who act too gay."

Damir nods knowingly. They sit in silence, vaguely moving to the music drifting from the stairwell, an old Pet Shop Boys number. Then they're all exchanging glances as the lyric sinks in: *Everything I ever do / Everywhere I'm going to / It's a sin.*

Mirza can't place Lola's accent. He asks if Bosnia is her home.

"Zagreb, but I went to school in Germany. I live in Dubrovnik mostly. Damir said you're from Toronto."

"Yep, but here too. I grew up in Kovači. We left in ninety-six." Mirza sees the change in Lola's eyes: the look people get when they think they see the war in your face. He says, "I was in Dubrovnik a few times when I was a kid. We always went to the coast in summer."

"You should come again. You can stay at my place. Damir has been there."

"Thank you. That'd be nice."

Lola gets up. "Boys, I gotta run. Need to find my girlfriend."

They drink more beer, dance till they are bathed in sweat. On the dance floor they meet Lola's girlfriend, whose bellowed name Mirza can't catch, then he and Damir head back to the terrace.

Mirza needs this night: too many beers, obliterating music, a night to push the real world out of his mind. His mother and Ćelo, the motel, those horrible men, a feeling like a stone dropping through his insides. He is inexpressibly glad that Damir is with him here. It is definitely feeling like a date now. They sit, cooling down at a terrace table, blearily watching the animated conversations around them. He feels Damir's leg press and hold against his own. Their eyes meet, which seems to demand a mutual laugh.

"It's a sin."

"Fuck you."

"Especially that."

Damir gets funnier when he drinks. He obviously hasn't sworn off booze for Ramadan. After sunset, it seems, the beer can flow.

"Will you come see me in Tuzla?"

"What about your roommate?"

"He goes to his parents on weekends, usually. But I can come here, if I don't have exams or whatever. When do you go to Toronto?"

"October. Soon."

"You will see your girlfriend?"
"What girlfriend?"
"Very good answer."

They walk back through Ferhadija and the shuttered marketplace to Kovači. By the tram loop two idle taxi drivers look right through them. Their secret is invisible. Mirza unlocks the flat and motions Damir ahead of him into the dark entryway. His father is in Višegrad and due back in the morning, which might mean as early as nine or ten. But why not let him see Damir here?

He clicks the door shut and turns around. Damir is right there, his heat and scent. Mirza gently pulls their bodies together and puts his lips to the salty tang of his friend's neck.

32

Pero still dreams of Mićo's death. The dreams are all mixed-up nonsense. But in Pero's memory the event itself remains clear. Šaban was altered by it. His fire dimmed, and it took weeks, months, to come back.

Their Brigade unit was stationed in the ruin of an inn on the square in Višegrad. They carted stones to help rebuild a blasted arch of the old bridge. They cleared debris of every kind in the town and surrounding region, anything from rubble to destroyed vehicles to the remains of dead horses. Once they had to pull corpses out of a pit where the Ustashas had thrown dozens of executed Partisans.

Šaban had been trained to scavenge parts from the engines of wrecked tanks and trucks. Mićo, an orphaned boy, took a fancy to him — or possibly just to the idea of having grease up to his elbows. Mićo began as a pest but became a kind of apprentice. Šaban seemed not to have the heart to tell him to get lost. The boy and his grandmother were billeted with refugees in the high school. Then the grandmother died, and on Šaban's initiative Mićo joined their Brigade cohort though he was not even old enough to shave. He moved into the inn with the rest of the comrades.

They had wanted to salvage a big armoured truck half submerged in the Drina. With horses and men, they dragged the wreck partway onto the sloping bank until it stopped and refused to go further. They heaved and sweated, the ropes cutting into their flesh, but the truck wanted only to roll back again into the river.

A shout went up: "Mićo, a rock, that big one! Jovo, help him! Under the wheel, quickly!"

Mićo and Jovo got the rock behind the rear wheel, but then it simply began to slide with the truck down the muddy bank as men and beasts lost the last of their strength. The boys scrambled again to push the rock against the wheel, and Mićo stumbled, then he was down and under the big double tires. The wheels went over him. He flipped up and was caught in the undercarriage, and he plunged with the truck into the swirling water.

His comrades dove in to find him. No one could. Šaban stayed until after dark, and Pero stayed with him and half drowned himself before giving up in utter fatigue, and still Šaban was going under and coming up gasping and spitting, countless times, until he too collapsed on the bank. They lay there half dead. Then shouting came from far down the river, where the others had found Mićo's body.

Pero's chest is bursting. It's as if his throat is packed full of mud and every lung-searing effort for air sucks the gunk deeper into him. He knows that he is dreaming and if only he can wake up he will breathe again. And wake he does with a massive in-rush of air pulled in through the mud plug. He lies on his back with his chest heaving, tears trickling down into his ears. Someone is standing over him.

"*Deda*, are you all right?"

"Mićo ..."

"There is no Mićo, *Deda*. It's Mirza. I'm back."

33

My sister is unable to pretend enthusiasm for her son's work. Mirza's MOCCA showcase will be up in a week. Krista did say she "hopes to attend" the opening, depending how she feels. She's been having headaches — a recurrence, it seems, of the migraines she had years ago, during and after the war. She told Mirza this via email, even though Mirza is here in Toronto and staying in my house a few blocks away.

Family complications aside, *Atrocity W/Rap* is in fact not the sort of art one can enthuse about. It needs some distance — and even then, for me, the times I've seen it have always triggered a kind of brain freeze. Burned and mangled bodies, impossibly upright, hobnobbing in shredded cocktail attire. It repels me. I stifle the thought, surely my own lapse, that it is itself a form of desecration. You can faintly smell the burn and the rot. (Mirza told me he used lamb's blood for some of the effects.) Knowing my nephew, I know his intent runs much deeper than a need to provoke. But will people (will critics) see that? Krista should probably stay away from the show, for Mirza's sake too.

Another factor: Mirza knows now about the motel. He told me what his father told him, and I had to say I knew it already from his mother. I've made sure he understands that what he heard is not what he was meant to know, that Adem was not supposed to speak about it. To this Mirza said, "He had to tell me. He still works with people who were there." That left me looking at the extent of my ignorance.

Mirza has been putting in twelve-hour days at his studio, the work apparently too intense to be discussed. He has seen his mother only twice in the two weeks since he returned. The day after Mirza arrived home, Kristina came by for dinner, but once the initial hugs were over, the strain set in. Whenever the real preoccupations surfaced — the upcoming show, Mirza and Bosnia, Adem — conversation stalled. Mirza and his mother talked vaguely around each other or went stone-faced while I tried to rally us back to trivial things. I sat there dreading that we'd stumble into the truly unspeakable. Pero ate with us and was uncharacteristically quiet. In the silences, we listened to his jaw clicking while he chewed.

I drove Krista home. As we sat by the curb outside her house she said, "I don't know them anymore. You're the only one I know."

❖

I spend an afternoon helping Mirza and his friend Teo transport the mannequins from his studio to the gallery space at MOCCA. The two of them are brisk and upbeat with each other, but it seems to me a thin cover. I remember Mirza saying there was some sort of artistic disagreement between them — which would be personal. And, of course, Teo is not part of the show.

Mirza has rented a cube van and movers' padding. Though the mannequins could each be disassembled under normal conditions, Teo's suggestion of this, as we stand in the studio assessing options, is met with reflexive dismissal from Mirza. He's obviously right. The sectional joints have been obliterated, probably fused together, by his work.

Mirza has a bolt of clear plastic sheeting. He explains: each figure must be gently wrapped in plastic, then swaddled in the padded blankets and tied securely. The three of us set to work on the first mannequin, a female with her eyes burned to black holes, her breasts two mounds of — I don't know what the material is, but it looks like decayed and blackened meat, part raw, part charred. The torso of one male is like a butchered carcass. Mirza has managed to make the hacked flesh look wet with pink and yellowish ooze. Teo mentions resin and something else, and Mirza nods.

He has supplied us with cotton gloves. He indicates where we should grasp the figures while he deals with the wrap and padding. His face is tight with worry. Parts of the mannequins and their clothing are caked with what looks like dried shit, which may be the lamb's blood. Scraps of the substance slough off the figure that we're presently wrapping. Mirza swears quietly, staring at the crumbled bits on the floor. Teo asks if a spray coat of laquer would help, and Mirza gives the idea a long, anxious stare. "Tomorrow," he says. He will have all day to fiddle, before the opening party at six p.m.

MOCCA is perhaps a ten-minute drive from Mirza's studio, but it takes us two trips and over five hours to get all sixteen figures settled in the showcase gallery with their wrappings removed, skewed limbs repositioned, stray parts reattached. The staff assisting on-site watch with interest as the wraps come off. Observing what moves through their faces, it seems the figures are what Mirza means them to be: ghastly, intriguing, discombobulating. People linger and gawk. Mirza moves back for a long look, then walks among the massacred. It's crucial that there be enough elbow room so the public can mingle. Amid all his fussing and adjusting and protectiveness, Mirza has a subtle glow. Teo is taking notice; I see the mix of respect and envy sparring inside him.

In a pub on Queen Street near MOCCA we're on our first pints, much deserved. Teo, his duty done, has departed. Mirza is showing me pictures on his phone of Damir, his new/old Sarajevo friend. Damir sports longish chestnut-brown hair and a slightly crooked smile. He looks younger, by a bit.

"He was a neighbour. They came from Višegrad. They had it worse than us."

"Hard to believe."

"Nobody was killed in our family. My uncle Medo, but I barely knew him."

"And *Deda*. And your mother."

Mirza stares at me.

"I mean, not killed but ..." I can't finish.

"It was worse for Damir. Honestly."

He scrolls through the shots, turns the display to me with a wry look: Adem at a stove with a kitchen implement in hand.

"Yes, he's cooking. Eggs and sausage, that's his limit."

More scrolling, more shots of Damir. In one he is posed next to a gruesome-looking charred animal skull, the eyeballs white as boiled eggs. A man in a stained apron is grinning in the background.

"Farmers' market. They sell baked sheep heads." Mirza sips his beer. "We didn't buy one."

His face flickers with contentment as he moves through the pictures.

"Are you lovers?"

Mirza looks at me: "Yeah. I guess we are."

"He looks very sweet."

"He is. Smart too."

"That would go without saying. How will you stay in touch?"

"I'm going back. Once the show is down."

"Will you be able to work?"

"I'm already working for my father. But I could work, sure. I'm a Bosnian citizen."

"What happened with your other friend? Kemo?"

"He's an Islamist. He's telling his sister how to dress."

"Oh dear."

"He could not by any stretch be my boyfriend. Even if he was gay, he would have to pretend he isn't."

"A fundamentalist tradition."

Mirza pockets his phone. Staring into his beer, he says, "Do you think my mother will come tomorrow?"

"I doubt it. I think, honestly, she should stay away."

"Did you tell her that?"

"Would you like me to?"

Mirza gives me a naked look. "I emailed her yesterday. I told her she was welcome, that I'd like to see her but I'd understand completely if she can't."

"I'm glad you did that. Did she reply?"

"She said, 'I'll try to be there.'

34

It was inevitable. The word comes from a knot of people over by the food table: *zombies.* A woman's voice, amused. Mirza dismisses the thought. Has he ever actually seen a zombie movie? *Night of the Living Dead*, an old black and white thing. The title sits stupidly in his mind as he scans his own living dead. They are both more real and less real than latexed, gore-smeared actors lurching through graveyards. A moment later the word comes again: from a rotund man with a goatee — not by any stretch a hip goatee. It's a Burl Ives goatee. He's beside a somewhat younger woman with long, straight, cranberry-coloured hair. Mirza comes up beside them and starts talking.

"The zombie thing is inevitable isn't it? I had clips running at one point, stuff out of horror films, looped really tight so it became inane — almost laughable, you know?" The two are nodding pensively at him. "Video seemed wrong. Too much. And too inter-genre. Laughable was wrong, definitely, I mean that kind of filmic, slapstick comedy. There's an edge, a thin edge, between seeing the farce, and madness. I mean the kind of farce or madness that comes from living in a war zone."

"As you did," says the goatee.

"As I did, yes, in Sarajevo."

"You are Mirza ...?"

"Osmanović."

The man says, "I'm from Belgrade, in fact, a long time ago. And so is Biljana."

Biljana says, "Not so long ago for me. And Lazo, you forget, I'm not from Belgrade."

He laughs. "Yes, I'm wrong. It was ...?"

"Vukovar. I received my doctorate in Belgrade."

They all stand nodding.

Mirza will not ask what sort of doctor she is. He says, "I experimented with clips from the war. TV news. But ..."

Lazo's brows go up. "Too specific?"

"Exactly."

"A fine line isn't it? Between art and propaganda. An obvious line, actually. Were your war clips from Sarajevo?"

"Srebrenica. I was there, this summer."

"Of course. For research?" says Lazo in Serbian.

"*Točna.*"

"*Naravno. Autentičnost.*"

Lazo's tone sounds subtly mocking in his native language. He tilts his head and continues in Serbian, "The Potočari site is quite beautiful, don't you think? All of those lovely gravestones in perfect rows. It is indeed a wonderful sight to behold, the purity of that Austrian marble. It's clear everyone is going to heaven, yes?" He smiles. "And the big slab at the entrance. The number carved there permanently. Eight thousand three hundred and something, I don't know what. But they know. It's an exact number. It's in stone now, so schoolchildren can write it down for eternity. But it is inflated, by as much as one hundred per cent. The fact is they carved the number even before they counted all the bodies, even before they determined, in some cases, whose bodies they were digging up." Lazo is still smiling.

"It's not about Srebrenica. That's why I didn't use the video, ultimately."

"But you have handed out these invitations, from the ..." He reads from his card: "*The Office of the High Investigator* and the *Research and Identification Commission*."

"People may infer something. There's no reference anywhere to Srebrenica or Bosnia."

"Only your name. Your origin."

"My father is Muslim, but my mother isn't."

The cranberry hair says, "And she suffered in the war as well."

Mirza stares at them. They are cooly waiting.

"She suffered. She still does. We were in the siege."

"She must find your work difficult," says the woman, watching him intently.

Mirza suddenly wants to strangle her. He wants to set her shiny, perfectly ironed hair on fire. He feels his face heating up.

She repeats, "Difficult. Our history."

Lazo says, "I want a little more wine," and he leaves.

The woman doesn't budge: "Is your mother here today?"

"I need some wine too. Enjoy the show."

Mirza heads toward the wine bar. His mother hasn't shown, and he's already feeling the relief of this, mixed with a fear that she's on the way. By the bar he sees the goatee jawing away at someone and glancing at his approach. Mirza veers off, moves to join the people walking among his figures.

What the killings, the wars, mean to him personally is not the point, or is only one among a universe of points. He will say this, analyze this, when interviewed by the media. Of course, he may only be interviewed by bloggers and arts journals. But Lydia Rajak says the piece could go elsewhere, maybe even the National Gallery, maybe Europe.

Another artist with work in the show, a painter he dated once, before Jen, is wandering among the dead. From the wall opposite, her huge pastel nudes observe Mirza's carnage from their blossoming flower faces. Rachel now stops beside one of the male mannequins: a waiter, and the only figure positioned flat out on the floor, his tray and spilled spring rolls beside him. Mirza has given the otherwise impeccable waiter a gaping head wound and an accompanying chicken. It was not easy to find a realistic chicken. He finally had to buy a real one and pay a taxidermist. The hen is pecking at the waiter's smashed skull. In its bloody beak is a chunk of what could be brain matter. He has watched people gripped by fascination and revulsion at the waiter tableau.

Rachel says, "Hmm. I don't know what to say."

"Say it. It's like Alfred Hitchcock. That evil bird movie."

"*The Chickens.*"

"That would be the Mel Brooks version."

Rachel considers: "No, they were pigeons, weren't they?"

"Maybe. Anyway, conceptually, a chicken is the only choice here."

"Because we eat them."

"On one level. And there's a historical reference."

"Why do you make the mass grave thing so specific?" She reads from her invitation card: "*The Southeast Exhumation Quadrant of the Republic.*"

"How is it specific? You mean to war, to war crimes?"

"Well, to where you're from. To Bosnia."

"It doesn't say Bosnia. Only in my bio."

Rachel examines the card. "But where you're from matters."

"It sure fucking does, doesn't it?"

"Never mind. I'm sorry."

"Don't be sorry. Really. I'm not —" Rachel is eyeing him with touching sympathy. He can understand why she paints what she does. He says, "It does matter. It matters to me, it matters to a lot of people, but I'm not interested in the ethnic narrative, the media spin that people jump to every time the — you know, who did what, who killed who. I think I have to keep the specifics out of it." He stops to breathe. Rachel is nodding agreement without looking at all convinced. Mirza hasn't fully convinced himself. "It would be nice, I suppose, if I could do your paintings. I mean, if I was actually capable of that. They're probably going to sell out."

"I sold one already."

"Right. But it's not in me to create those pictures. I mean, I understand them. I actually think of people that way, of their flowering, their fragility. Their beautiful nakedness." Mirza realizes that he means this, means it deeply. "It's even appropriate that we're in the same show, you know? Beauty and the beast." He forces a smile.

"Sure. Yes. I get that."

Mirza sees his uncle Alex by the far entrance, with his mother and Lydia Rajak. He excuses himself from Rachel, gets a wine refill, and heads over to them. Lydia is talking intently to his uncle. Mirza's mother is slack-faced and silent, staring at

Lydia with a dull effort of concentration. Is she drunk? Thankfully, she has no wine at the moment. Alex looks stressed. Lydia, motor-mouthing, is simply pretending Kristina doesn't exist.

"... and of course I've suggested to the artist — hello, Mirza — that we get a complete photo and video record before the show comes down, with an artist interview."

"I was just interviewed over there, by creepy Belgraders."

"Lazo."

"Lazo, yes. Who is he?"

"He has a gallery in Burlington. He's not significant. I must go and chat with your fans. The turnout is encouraging, yes? You seem to be the star, not surprisingly."

Lydia purposefully moves off, her wine hoisted. Mirza turns to see his mother coming at him. She leans in, gives him a peck on the cheek.

"The star. Well."

She is wearing a dress he hasn't seen in years, a deep green, shimmering satin item that shows off her wide, almost masculine shoulders. He has always liked it, and it still looks striking on her. She wore it for him, and she is even smiling for him now but somehow with her lips down-turning, crushed together. Her eyes are lifeless.

"That woman ... she's ..."

"Lydia, my agent."

"Mm ..." Her gaze wanders the room. Mirza sees her eyes take in his installation for a few seconds and then sprint away. She turns and observes the wall hung with Rachel's benign nudes.

"Mother?"

"Lovely. They have flower heads."

"I'm glad you're here."

"I need to sit down."

Then she is on the floor before they can react. Mirza and Alex go down to catch her at the last moment as she slumps. They ease her down onto the hard parquet, her eyes rolling up into her head. People are gasping. A few rush to help as the party chatter stalls, then slowly returns. His mother is completely limp, motionless. Her head is as heavy as a stone, her eyes wide open and full white. Mirza pulls his phone out as someone hands him a glass of water. He gives the phone to Alex and cradles his mother's head, puts the water to her lips, but she is unresponsive.

35

A doctor is in front of us, young and smooth-faced and hair-gelled. He perches on the edge of the waiting room chair as if indicating his duty to move on.

"You're the husband?"

"I'm her brother. Mirza here is her son."

"It appears your mother mildly overdosed on prescription drugs. We think it was accidental. An anti-depressant, along with an opiate, which she was carrying. And, it seems, some alcohol. Has she been under stress lately?"

Mirza looks helplessly at me.

I tell the doctor, "There was a trigger, an event, tonight."

The doctor glides on. "The dosage was not terribly high judging from blood results. It's largely the combination with alcohol. I'd suggest she have a talk with her doctor, or doctors. She may be over-prescribed. She mentioned a psychiatrist."

"Yes."

"We'd like to keep her overnight. We're waiting on some more tests just to be safe. You can see her now. Through those doors and follow the yellow arrows. Someone will help you."

As we get up Mirza says, "She's seeing a psychiatrist?"

"She said she might. I don't know."

Krista's smiles tiredly as we approach her bed.

"I'm all right. I just got off track a bit. I'm sorry, Mirza."

"No worries. I'm glad you came. I'm sorry this happened."

"Your work seems to be a success."

"Me and a few others."

"You don't need to tell your father about this."

"I won't."

"Or you, Alex."

"No. No need."

"I'm glad for you, Mirza. Maybe it doesn't seem ..." Her mouth twists.

"It's good. It's fine. Please don't worry."

"I didn't intend — well, so much drama."

She gives a faint smile. We sit through a silence. Mirza reaches and rests his hand on his mother's. The gesture is tender, but the hands pose stiffly until Mirza pulls away.

A nurse comes to take more blood. Mirza and I part in the corridor. I've encouraged him to get back to his show; I will stay with his mother until they get her settled. We hug, and I go back to Kristina. Her bed is curtained off from the six or eight others in the large room, and when I part the curtain, her back is to me, her blue gown gaping open to show white underpants and her naked spine as she goes through the plastic bag containing her clothes. Her search seems slightly frantic.

"Krista."

"Yes!" She turns. "You startled me. I can't find my pills."

"They must have them."

"I need them."

"Well, I'll see what I can —"

"Get them. Please get them," she says, her mouth taut.

I turn around and go back to the nursing station.

"My sister is wanting her drugs, her anti-depressants, I guess. I'm not sure."

"Her name?"

"Kristina Osmanović. She seems pretty desperate."

The nurse gives me hard look. "Okay, sir, I'll check her status. Did you want to go back to her?"

"Yes, yes."

I hurry back. The woman in the bed nearest Krista's has a visitor, a man in a suit who turns to me and says, "Are you the brother? I'm sorry, would you control her, please? She went through my mother's things."

I pull the curtain aside. Krista is on the edge of the bed. She is weeping without sound. Her mouth is a gaping hole. I sit and put an arm around her, and then the sound comes: a howl. I hug her, make tender noises, but the horrible wailing doesn't stop.

Mirza cabs back to the gallery and is duly surrounded by a knot of concern. Lydia, Teo, Rachel, event staffers. He tells them his mother mixed a prescription drug with a bit too much wine. "She's just been a little stressed," he says lightly. "They say she'll be fine. Maybe should have stayed home, but, hey, she's my mom." The faces around him flash relieved smiles. Someone says, "You probably want some wine," and Mirza says, "Glass of red. Full!" People drift off, party selves restored.

The room is loud and frenetic, almost packed now. Patrons bray and drink and graze the remains at the canapé table. In singles or little groups they gravely commune with Mirza's horrors, gaze serenely at Rachel's peach-toned flower people, ponder the abstract canvasses and metallic sculptures of the two other artists. He catches sight of Lazo and the cranberry lady studying a small canvas in an alcove, as if the point is to show their backs to the featured art.

Mirza's wine arrives, in Teo's hand.

"Full up, as requested."

They clink, sip, swallow.

"So, for real, is she okay?"

Mirza looks at Teo. "It's tough for her. I don't

know why she came."

"That's what mothers do."

Is there a hint of reproach in Teo's voice? They both look away. The director of MOCCA, also curator of the showcase, is moving among the atrocities with Mirza's agent. The two women are a picture of serious engagement. Mirza can't help thinking that a deal of some sort is being forged. And meanwhile Teo is judging him: the bad son, the callous careerist, or whatever he needs to think to be reassured about his own work, his choices. They've always been rivals, the way all friends are on some level. But right now there is nothing they can say about it, and they shouldn't try.

Teo says it anyway: "What's with the chicken? You didn't have that a week ago."

Mirza looks at him. "I'm sorry? *What's with the chicken?* Am I supposed to have a short answer for that?"

"Give me the long and intense answer."

"Give me yours."

Teo looks at him for a moment, a very long moment. His jaw is working: "It just seems — I have to say it — it seems gratuitous."

"Really. Like a canvas with three bars of colour on it and nothing else."

"What?"

"Like Christ in a bottle of urine. Right? Like the Queen on a moose, or a shark in formaldehyde."

"Don't be such a dick."

"That you can even talk this way is the whole story."

"What whole story?"

"There it is again. Your fucking obliviousness."

"Careful, Miki ..."

"You're the guy who failed to be careful."

"I'm oblivious? I was in Mostar for fuck's sake, and you call me oblivious?"

"I'm talking about now, about the work. You just don't get the process, the evolution of a concept. That's why you stopped painting. Because at some point, you understood your limits."

Mirza instantly knows the bridge he has crossed. Teo looks struck, his mouth slack. He looks at the floor. Mirza watches his eyes shifting. He looks up with a curling grin.

"Come on, Miki — a chicken? A dead waiter with a chicken?"

Mirza walks away.

36

Mirza wakes in the night with his face wet, his pillow damp. The flow from his eyes is unconnected to any thought, the runoff from a dream he has no memory of. He gets up and wanders to the kitchen, opens the fridge, but it's not food he wants. He goes and sits in Alex's living room in the dim glow from the street lights. He feels blank, then the day tumbles back to him, and the tears come again.

In the morning, next to the pre-prepped coffee maker, he finds a note from his uncle saying he's at the hospital. It's disturbing what Alex told him late last night — about his mother's behaviour, her misery, their decision to keep her there longer. Alex's presence through all of this is actually keeping Mirza sane. He knows too that Alex has become an anchor for his mother, the rock that Mirza himself can't be. Turning on the coffee machine, with the clean mug set out beside it as always, Mirza is hit with gratitude.

He googles *mirza mocca toronto*. A blogger for an influential arts and culture magazine has reviewed the showcase. Mirza skims through the text until he sees his name:

> Mirza Osmanović takes a darker beast by the horns. While Rachel Gellert's work celebrates the gentle soul within, Osmanović has chosen to exorcise his demons through black satire and an unblinking dedication to the grisly — the palpable exhumation of memory. The installation of mutilated upright human forms is introduced through invitation cards offered by smiling attendants. This array of decay and horror is gathered for a cocktail event celebrating *"the successful completion of forensic excavation and analysis in the Southeast Exhumation Quadrant of the Republic."* These are the dead of mass graves.
>
> Point taken, glass of Pinot in hand, you wander among the human carnage, noting the disjunction of mind-numbing atrocity overlaid onto the smug indifference of commerce. Osmanović's medium is the ka-ching of global shill. His blasted and burned flesh (some of it gag-inducingly convincing) is seared into the plastic skins of fashion dummies.
>
> There are multiple messages here, not

all of them cohering, and the agitprop thrust is a tad too blunt — but there is no denying the bracing shock and lasting come-away power. Osmanović, whose childhood was spent in war-torn Bosnia, makes war enter your head to bang around against the urban complacent, where conflict rarely means more than a rude teen on the streetcar or a drug dealer shot in someone else's neighbourhood. *Atrocity W/Rap* may bray a touch too loudly with its clever title and cocktail bling, but the deeper substance of the show is stunning, disorienting in the best way. Osmanović is courting curators, not the living rooms of Rosedale. Let's hope the arbiters bite.

Mirza's heart is still pumping from dread. He has to read the review again to reassure himself. It's good. A touch snarky, but really good. Rachel has done well too (the writer is absolutely right that Rosedale is her market), but the other two artists are skimmed over, almost a tag end after Mirza's triumph. His title is lame, he knows it, but there is nothing condescending in the review. He is approached as an artist, not as some novice in training. He rereads and feels better each time.

He checks the MOCCA site, also Lydia's. Neither seems to have posted links to the review yet. He emails the gallery media person, then sends the review link to Lydia, his uncle, a few friends, and Damir. He sends it to his father, along with a note saying he will be back in Bosnia sometime soon, after the show comes down. He's now thinking that Bosnia's National Gallery might be interested, or the Sarajevo art academy.

He will not send the review to his mother. Later this afternoon he will drop by to see her.

37

I called in to Kristina's office first thing this morning and learned they were dismayed but not surprised by my news. She has recently been missing days at work. The woman I spoke to showed only concern for her health. We talked about making her absence official: a medical leave if needed. I said we would let them know.

Krista is beside me now, both of us in vinyl-covered armchairs in the patient lounge of the psychiatric wing. They want to get her reassessed and settled on whatever regimen is indicated. They are suggesting a stay of a few days to a week, depending how things go. I've brought in some toiletries and more comfortable clothes for her.

"Charming decor."

Krista looks blankly at me, then I get a faint smile. We settle to silence again, watching the to-and-fro of other patients and the images on a TV bolted high on the wall. There is just enough volume for the trashy talk show to lend a completely inappropriate ambience to the room.

Krista turns to me: "Did you see Mirza?"

"We spoke. He's coming by later."

"How did the show go?"

"All-round success I think."

"I'm in the lurch, aren't I?"

"What do you mean?"

"I suppose it's self-imposed. Why can't I support him like an ordinary mother? Why can't I adjust? Honestly, I just wish it would all go away. But it can't, and there's nothing I can do."

"We're with you utterly, Krista. All of us."

"You, yes. Mirza, yes, underneath I know that. Adem isn't with me. He has washed his hands of me. He's to blame for this."

"Can you blame one person? Surely the war is to blame. Adem was in it too."

She looks at me: "Don't tell me that. For God's sake, Alex. That he had it bad too?"

"All right. I'm sorry."

"That's completely beside the point. Completely. He aligned himself with the wrong people, from the beginning, criminals, and when they —" She stops, stares starkly, then she gets out of her chair. I follow her to the exit and tag along behind as she moves along the corridor to her room, staff and patients glancing at her face. At the door she halts. Her roommate has visitors. She turns and pushes me out of the way, finds a door and disappears behind it — a staff washroom. I hear the bolt snap shut. Uselessly, I try the doorknob. I knock, gently saying her name. There is a long silence, then a wail starts, rising in waves. I hear glass shatter. Down the hall I see a nurse pick up the phone.

Security staff comes, two young guys in cop-like uniforms with equipment hanging from their belts. They open the washroom door for me and a male nurse. Krista is down among shards of mirror on the floor. She is writhing, a creature of naked misery. Her hands are flecked with blood. The guards stand over me and the nurse as we try to calm her. She will not be calmed. She rears up and begins to hit out at us, cracking the nurse hard in the face. The guards catch her wrists in their latexed hands. She shrinks from them, wedging herself between wall and toilet. They grip her as she flails and screams, screams now because they are terrifying her, until a needle goes into her arm and within minutes she is only softly moaning, ready for the gurney waiting outside the door.

I have had a difficult few hours with the staff. Once Krista was immobilized in bed, I demanded to see the unit director. Later (when they'd rallied a defence, I assume) she met me. I asked why it was necessary right off the mark to call in security, whose presence put Krista in a state of terror they should have anticipated. Did they not know her history? I used the word *assault*. The director's response, in exactly the calm inflections I couldn't muster, was that Krista had assaulted the nurse before the guards laid a hand on her. She'd drawn blood: both her own, and the nurse's from a split lip.

"It's unfortunate," said the woman from behind her desk, "but your sister was a hazard to herself and our staff. Please understand. If things had escalated, we'd be liable."

This left me speechless, or rather, stifling the urge to say something stupid. I bit my tongue and walked away. Back in Krista's room, now a private one, I considered her bandaged hands and bruised arms. As I gradually calmed I noticed that the nursing staff, the rank and file, were making an extra effort.

Mirza calls in the evening to say he's ten minutes away. I hover at the nursing station to intercept him as he comes in. Krista is awake now, still woozy from whatever they've given her, but she left me in no doubt that I was not to tell Mirza or Adem the news about her breakdown. In fact, I've already misled Mirza. On the phone to him afterward I'd soft-pedalled the incident, deleting the broken glass, the guards, the violence and desperation, succumbing to the same protective impulse that urged him back to the gallery party last night: no worries, come when you can, Uncle is taking care of things. In any case, I was incapable of expressing to him what I'd witnessed.

Now Mirza is approaching me from the elevators with a wish-I-could've-been-here face, and all I can think of is the shock he will feel on seeing his mother's hands wrapped in gauze, the bruises, her face blank with sedation.

"Uncle. Sorry. I've been running non-stop all day. How's she doing?"

"This way." I steer him into a short hallway with "quiet" rooms. I sit him down and tell him what happened, not every detail because I can't, because it's too much: the crisis I triggered with my insensitive words, the terrible washroom scene, the pitch of madness she was driven to.

We go to Krista's room. She has dozed off. We pull up chairs and sit, Mirza by his mother's pillow. He stares, takes it in, turns to me with a defenceless look.

"Her hands."

"The broken mirror."

Mirza turns back to his mother. He leans close and says quietly, "Mom." No response. "Mama."

Kristina wakes up. She turns her head to him. She raises a tentative hand, then closes her lids as she sees the bandages. She lies still a few moments before mumbling, her eyes still shut, "I'm glad you're here."

"I came as soon as I could."

"Yes."

A silence. Then Krista says, "I need some water."

I hand Mirza the plastic cup. He adjusts her pillow and holds the cup so she can sip from the straw. When she's done, another long silence. She dozes again.

Mirza says to me, "You go. I can stay."

"You're sure? I don't mind."

"You've been here all day, Uncle."

We sit and watch her. I have never seen my sister look so old. Her breathing is all but imperceptible.

I say, "I called COSTI. Someone will come round tomorrow, a psychologist from her trauma group."

"Okay. That'll be good."

"They'll know what's best. Maybe get her out of here sooner."

"It's a drug problem, right? What happened today."

I'm at a loss to respond to this. It barely scratches the surface.

Mirza adds, "I mean, a better diagnosis ..."

"Should help, I suppose. Yes."

I don't move. It's as if the vinyl of the chair has fused to my backside.

"Go, Uncle."

"Right." I heave myself up. "Mirza, it's probably important that you not talk, I mean, that the two of you not discuss ..."

"The stuff we don't discuss. Yeah."

I glance at my watch. It's after seven p.m. "Did you eat? I can bring you a sandwich."

"I'm good."

"There's some mushroom risotto in the fridge, when you come in. And whatever."

"Great. Go, Uncle. *Go*."

I toddle out. Released.

38

"*Jebeni rat*," says my father flatly at breakfast, as if he is years beyond any recycling of emotion on the subject: *Fucking war.* He has patched a piece of his memory loop into what I just told him about his daughter's hospitalization: her own memory problem. He listens, chews and swallows his bite of toast and jam, then out come the two clipped words, then in goes more toast.

A phone message came while I was showering. There seems to be medical consensus on Krista: a drug imbalance plus an acute relapse of post-traumatic stress. The plan: fix the drug regimen, get her into ongoing therapy, and she should come back to herself, more or less. Mirza and I have agreed that the art must not be referred to. If she asks about it, short answers are best. Further discussion falls into the therapy realm. Mirza, I presume, has become his own therapist. We have seen the inside of his head.

My father begins to speak. He seems actually to be talking to me, filling me in. The content is familiar, but the words have a pitch I'm not used to, or perhaps I'm only listening more than usual.

"They went to hell and back, the ones who fought. Or they just died there. Or they came home, but they were — still out there. They talked about it sometimes. Late, with a fire, some drink in them. Telling us what happened. How a man was roasted. Pulled his liver out."

"*Tata*, please."

"Locked up a whole village of women and kept them for pleasure. What they did was shaming. Shame was in their faces when they told us, some of them. Others, they had smiles. They were victors. Me, I always loved women. I loved Mara."

"Mara, yes. She was your wife, *Tata*. My mother. And Krista's mother."

My father glances at me, then his gaze goes far away: "Mara ..."

He is motionless. Only the blinking, then the small brimming spill from his lids, down his leathery cheeks, dripping from stubbled chin. I get out of my chair and clear away his plate and mug, giving him the moment.

A bit later, he barks, "I went to the depot to join up. They laughed in my face. Rajko strutting around like a little fascist. They grabbed me and dragged me to the shed at the back, the pumphouse ..."

I do the washing up, tuning him out, thinking of what I might bring to the hospital for Krista. Should I bring our father? I look at him jawing away.

"*Tata? Tata?*" He's completely ignoring me. "Pero! Shut it!"

He stiffens, lifts his chin in defiance.

"Please. Silence now. Here, look at your photos." I take down the big holiday album and set it beside him.

39

We have been splitting the days into shifts with a few of Krista's long-time friends from COSTI. This afternoon Mirza is with his mother. I'm tidying while my father sleeps. It appears that Pero has stopped breathing: the strange apnea hiatus. He refuses to wear the anti-snore device. He lies very still as I gather together the pages of his memoir. I'm thinking we must get it properly bound when I find an odd piece: a page torn neatly from a book. A twitch of annoyance runs through me. This is from the skull novel, *The Excavations* — the copy, long overdue, that I returned to the TPL only yesterday. Pero has marked off a block of the text in pencil:

> In Serbia, not long ago, a young woman's body was found: the husk of Ana Mladić. Ana's father was at that point engaged in the elimination of thousands of Bosnian people he didn't like, in the belief that these peasants and professors and file

clerks would someday conquer and enslave Bosnia and then all of Europe. This bereaved father-warrior, Ratko, took some time off to be devastated by his daughter's suicide. Beside himself with rage and sorrow, he then returned with greater zeal to the task of killing thousands more.

It is said that a home video of Ana's funeral was later confiscated in a raid by secret police. It is said that Ratko's private grief over his daughter's coffin can now be purchased through certain illicit media channels. But why should we wish to see a butcher's grief? Or why not?

Pero has thickly underscored the words *beside himself* and *why*. I consider my sleeping father. The mystery of him. He is still eerily quiet. I gently shake his shoulder to bring on the explosive intake that will prove him still alive.

I don't give a fuck about Ratko's grief. I would tie Ratko Mladić to a chair in an abandoned factory. I would leave him there for, say, a month. He could have water and bland food, and a means of going to the toilet. For the entire month, with daily five-hour breaks for sleep or contemplation, I would play for him at ordinary volume, as if from a nearby room, the screams of the tortured. This would alternate every hour with Frank Sinatra's recording of "My Way," loud. Daily, at random times, I would have a gun put to Ratko's head. The gun would contain bullets and empty chambers. A bullet or two would first be fired into the ceiling. Bits of debris would fall onto Ratko. Then the gun would be held to Ratko's head and fired, or sometimes not fired. He would never actually be shot. The remaining bullets would be fired into the ceiling.

I lie awake sometimes and imagine this Ratko scenario. I have imagined similar things — frankly, worse things — for the men who hurt my sister.

I'm going now to see Krista. Mirza said she seems a little better today. The women from COSTI have been a godsend. Bosnia has come to consume my life. I knew on some level that I would not escape it. I was spared; now I'm summoned.

40

Mirza's installation is down and in storage. The show has generated four online reviews and one in a national newspaper. Three of the five notices are essentially raves and two are mixed (in Mirza's view, uncomprehending). Fortunately, the national newspaper review is an unqualified rave. His agent tells him that *Atrocity W/Rap* has a future. This seems to mean sometime next year at the earliest, which leaves Mirza free to think about how to refine the work.

He is in fact thinking about this right now, sitting on a café terrace by the Mostar bridge. Maybe — he can't imagine how yet, but he wants to try — maybe somehow, subtly, he can insert a glimmer of light. Not hope, exactly. Is there hope in *Guernica*, in those screaming horses and mothers? There is a light somewhere, held by someone. A hard light. All it does is illuminate.

"Hey." Damir is grinning at him.

"What?"

"Close your mouth."

"I was thinking."

"Never mind that. You look like you're in pain."

"I wasn't."

"Be here," says Damir, spreading his arms to take in the terrace and everything else, the river gorge and the arching bridge and blue sky. He has a wisp of cappuccino foam on his upper lip.

"I *was* here," he tells Damir. "Metaphorically."

"Ohhh. The artist speaks."

"Stop."

"Speak!"

Damir's face: The tilting grin, dark-chocolate eyes, traces of teenage blemish on his cheeks, the ridge of brow Mirza finds so appealing, the hair, great hair, thick and fine. It musses beautifully. Damir is perfect right now, though annoying.

Their eyes drift to contemplating the scenery: the restored bridge, aquamarine river, stone buildings that seem rooted to bedrock. The bridge is a revelation. To Mirza, the grace of the single Turkish arch, the purity of form and line substance, seem amazing, as amazing as its destruction, which he won't think about.

Damir flips up his hoodie.

"Do you want to go in?"

"No, the sun is perfect."

Even now, mid November, the air is mild, the tourists still coming. Mirza watches the figures mount the bridge span from either side. People concentrate loosely at the apex, pointing their cameras down the gorge. It seems to him that right now nothing is missing. He doesn't even want another coffee. He's not even wanting Damir. He has Damir. What they might have or not have, later, seems meaningless.

"How is your mother doing? Better?"

Mirza won't let this question bring them down. Everyone says stay positive. It helps, but he has to keep reminding himself: fighting his mother is wrong. It's just fighting himself in another way, a way that hurts them both. He has sometimes been heartless. It has helped lately to just keep things light. When he speaks to her on the phone, he talks about the summer house or the weather or Uncle Alex. And about Damir.

"Better. She's getting better. For sure. She has a good therapist. Great support. My uncle is incredible, and her women's group. She's back to work now, I think, or soon. We're supposed to spend a few weeks on the coast in April."

"I remember her, kind of. Bringing food to us."

"You'll see her in April. She will like you. If you don't talk about Allah."

"Please. When do I talk about Allah?"

"Hardly ever. But don't. She might think you're like Kemo."

"Give me some credit."

"I should."

"Give *your mother* some credit."

They will have dinner later, an early night, then up with the sun and a two-hour drive to Dubrovnik, to Damir's friend Lola. A few days at Lola's beach house, then they will head up the coast to Makarska. They will join Adem for some reno work at the summer house Mirza hasn't seen since childhood. He will also see his paternal grandmother again, finally. And then of course next spring, when they will all be together there — Damir too, he hopes. Mirza will not mention his work. It will be a holiday.

On nights they share in the Kovači apartment, when his father is away, Mirza sometimes wakes in an empty bed and goes out to find Damir on the sofa with his knees to his chest, folded up. Just a touch from Mirza's hand can break the silence that's been held and then Damir bawls like a child. He never wakes Mirza. Mirza wakes from feeling the absence. It's a whole new kind of comfort, holding Damir in the dark at these moments. There is nothing better.

A note on language

The Bosnian characters in *Makarska* all communicate in the same Slavic language, but readers will notice that they don't always call it by the same name.

The question of how to designate the language spoken in Bosnia and Herzegovina is a contentious one. Before the wars of the 1990s, the term in general use by linguists was *Serbo-Croatian*. Some now prefer the more inclusive term, *Bosnian/Croatian/Serbian*. Others contend that it is not a single language at all. In actual practice, *Bosnian*, *Serbian*, and *Croatian* refer to minimal variants of the language understood in everyday usage by all South Slavs in Bosnia, Serbia, Croatia, and Montenegro.

Like many Bosnian families, the one in this novel is of mixed ethnicity. As individuals, they may refer to the language they speak by the name linking it to their ethnic or religious identity, or, depending on context, by the collective and more neutral term *Bosnian*.

JB

Acknowledgments

I am not Bosnian, and as far as I know, I have no Yugoslav ancestry. This book would not exist in its present form, or maybe not in any form, were it not for the human connections and friendships I have made, both in former Yugoslavia and in Canada. The list below is incomplete. It could include many more whose insights or kindnesses were helpful even if fleeting.

Višnja Brčić; Goran Simić; Goran Ćirić; Edin Bajrić; Lydia Perović; Emina Trumić; Mirza Beširović; Amila Hrustić; Peter Lippman; Mirsad Siručić and family; Beba Hadžić; Maja Špoljar; Sang Kim; Istok Bratić; Amela Marin; Svetlana Đurković; Alma Selimović; Jasmin Mujanović; Maki Žiško; Richard Fung; Miljan Vujević; Veba Božović; Colin Carberry; Zlata Filipović; Emir Suljagić; Amila Buturović; Karen Mulhallen; Tanya Pikula; Dragomir Ivković; Nihad Živojević; Draško Bogdanović.

A revised version of Chapter 16 appeared in the 2012 "Bosnia" issue of *Descant Magazine*, edited by Amila Buturović.

I'm grateful to my editor at Insomniac Press, Gillian Rodgerson, for her unflagging support, subtle understanding, and expert advice. Also to my dedicated and tenacious agent, Martha Webb of Anne McDermid & Associates.

Special thanks to my my partner, Brian Pronger, for gracefully enduring many years of my Yugoslav obsession, and to Dan Healey and Mark Cornwall for sharing Slavic insights and a memorable trip through Bosnia.

Funding from the Writers' Reserve program of the Ontario Arts Council, through the support of Quattro Books, House of Anansi Press, and the Porcupine's Quill, assisted in the completion of the manuscript.

Twitter fans can find Jim Bartley @bartleybabica.

Makarska
by Jim Bartley

Mirza has masqueraded as "Mickey" throughout his time in Canada, but his own identity awaits him when he returns to spend a summer in postwar Sarajevo with his father. His grandfather bears the physical scars of the violence. His mother's psychological wounds are hidden, but reopen when Mirza uses the war as inspiration for a new art installation.

Through the eyes of three generations, Jim Bartley's much anticipated second novel tells a tale at once sweeping and intimate, an unflinching story of war, escape, heart-rending loss, budding love, and the hard-won understanding that true escape is an elusive and lifelong project.

Jim Bartley is a novelist and playwright. He has written about books for *The Globe and Mail*, *National Post*, *Toronto Xtra*, and other publications. *Makarska*, and his first novel, *Drina Bridge*, grow out of his long interest in the lives and stories of people in Bosnia and former Yugoslavia. He lives in Toronto with his partner of thirty-eight years and a large black poodle.

CPSIA information can be obtained at www.ICGtesting.com
Printed in the USA
LVOW04s2107290615

444327LV00016B/192/P